THE CHILLED CORPSE

By

Louy Castonguay

Copyright © by Louy Castonguay. **ALL** Rights reserved Printed in the US. No part of this book may be used or reproduced in any manner whatsoever without written permission except in the case of brief quotations embodied in critical articles or reviews.

Contact Louy Castonguay at louycwriter123@gmail.com

Cover by Get Covers

This is a work of fiction. Any resemblance to any characters is accidental

The Chilled Corpse

Chapter 1

The phone woke Annie at nine. She'd overslept again. "Oh, Hi Josie. What's up?"

"Hey, Annie. You said you wanted cooking lessons?"

Annie had moved to the small town of Abigale less than a month ago, into a big old house left to her by her birth grandmother.

"I have guests. Two couples. I'll be doing up scones and biscuits for their breakfast for tomorrow. Want to learn?"

"Yes. But when?"

"When you get here. I'm in no hurry. But before noon. I'll be busy this afternoon, and this evening, as you know, is my Friday supper bash. I'll have a full house, then. So, sometime this morning. I always do them up and put them in the chill chest to set up and hydrate fully. Gives a lighter crumb." I'll bake them in the morning so's they're fresh.

"Lighter crumb. That's a good thing, I take it."

"Oh, yes. So, are you in?"

"Yes. Give me an hour?"

"You got it. I'll do up the dessert for tonight while waiting."

"Yes, and any more table reservations available?"

"Tom and Joe have a table. I can put you there, if you don't mind."

"That's fine. See you soon."

Annie jumped out of bed and got herself ready to go have a cooking lesson.

Louy Castonguay

Josie was setting up tables when she arrived at the inn. "Ah, there you are. And right on time."

Josie ran an inn, with meals for the public, with a very limited menu served buffet style on Friday evenings and sometimes on Saturdays. She also did lunch on Monday, Tuesday, Wednesday, and Saturday, with the cook's choice of only a few options.

Annie had never taken time to learn to cook and was eager to learn. "What sort of scone are we making?"

"I'll tell you. It's getting harder and harder to come up with stuff, if I want to please everyone, which I've decided not to. They can just skip it, if they wish. Lactose intolerant, gluten sensitive, vegetarian, vegan, or that new starch free one, caveman diet or whatever."

"What have you decided on for tonight?"

"Blond brownies with ice cream. It's easy to portion that out."

"Yummy. And will you show me how to do that, too?"

"Yes. It's simple. One of the easiest things. Can you make brownies?"

"Only time I tried, I failed. They were as hard as a rock."

"Ah, over cooked. Probably the oven was too hot."

"Show me. Scones, you said. That sounds complicated. And I have had no luck with biscuits, either."

"You go fetch the butter in the cooler while I set out the ingredients. My two couples came in last night and I heard them go out this morning, real early. I think they were going hiking."

"How much butter."

The Chilled Corpse   Page 3

"We'll need two pounds. One for the scones and one for the biscuits. I'll cook half of the biscuits for supper and half for breakfast tomorrow."

"Got it." Annie knew where the cooler was, though she'd never been in it.

She opened the door and halted two steps inside of the closest-sized walk in. She stared at the corner, where there was a bundle of rags, her mind refusing to tell her what was really there.

"Josie," she croaked, her throat suddenly dry. She tried again. "Josie!" Then again, more urgently, but no louder. "Josie." She backed up two steps and blinked her eyes, thinking she was seeing things. She took two more steps back, then whirled around, letting the door close behind her. She headed for the dining area, where Josie was setting up the cooking lesson. "Josie." Finally, much louder, as she entered the dining area. "Josie."

Josie looked up. "What. You couldn't find the butter? I know I have lots." She looked up at Annie. "You look like you've seen a ghost. Sit." She guided Annie to a chair. "Sit. My gosh, your' white as a sheet."

Annie shook her head, as she sat. "In your walk in. I think there's a man in there."

"Of course there isn't. You were seeing things." She put a hand on Annie shoulder. "The light in there isn't good and flickers."

"No. I think there's a dead man in your cooler."

"Can't be." She turned and stepped away from Annie and strode to the kitchen and to the walk in. One minute later, she came back to Annie. "You were right." She abruptly sat next to Annie and put a hand on her arm. "Oh, my gosh. Oh, my."

"Where's your phone."

"Oh, right. Phone." She picked up the phone from the table and dialed the sheriff. "Hey, Is Dave in?" She waited a moment. "No, Dave, please. Yes, it is urgent." Her voice was shaky and the deputy answering the phone must have picked up on that.

In a moment, Dave Frost, the Sheriff, answered and she told him what was going on. "I think it's one of my guests who checked in last night. Please, come over?" She nodded in agreement with him. "I'll be here. Annie is here with me. We were going to do a cooking lesson. Scones. She went to get the butter." She clamped her mouth shut to stop spewing words nervously.

"Is he coming?" Annie was trembling a little.

"Yes. He'll be here in just a few minutes."

Annie had a hand on the table and one on her heart.

Josie put her hand over the one on the table and the two were holding on to each other when the Sheriff arrived. He was tall and had only a slight belly, but was handsome in a mid-forties way in his starched brown uniform.

Annie found the glint on his pocket from his badge to be reassuring.

"In the cooler?"

"Yes," croaked Josie. "Annie was the first to find him. We haven't touched anything."

The Chilled Corpse   Page 5

Sheriff Dave strode to the back room. He came back a minute later. "Yup. Dead man in the cooler. A thoroughly chilled corpse you have there. You know who he is?"

"Gene Gent. Oh, gosh, that sounds like a made-up name. It's what he used to sign in. Him and three others. Two women, two men. I thought they looked like two couples."

"And where are the rest of them?"

"I heard them go out about seven this morning. I thought they'd all left. I didn't actually see them."

"Did they check out or go out for the day?"

"I didn't ---. I'll go look at the rooms, to see if they took their stuff." Josie stood as if to go look at the rooms.

"Leave it. I'll go have a look-see. This is all a crime scene, now."

"Oh, gosh. I won't be able to serve supper, will I. Do you suppose I'll have to throw out all the food in there?" Her eyes were dilated and huge. "Where did he die? Who killed him." She looked at the sheriff. "I didn't do it."

Annie looked at her and then the sheriff. "I didn't' do it either. I just got here."

Dave made a downward motion with his right hand. "Sit. We'll have to get the Staties in here."

"So, not natural causes, I take it?" Josie was still on the edge of her chair.

"No. He's got a knife in his heart."

"I didn't see blood," said Annie.

"No, the knife would have stopped the heart. Blood only flows when the heart is beating. But he may not have been killed there. We'll have to wait and see. I'm not equipped to do an investigation like this."

"Yes," said Josie, about nothing special. "I think I'll call Tom. Or should I call Joe? He's the lawyer."

Annie was starting to regain her senses after the shock. "Why not call both?"

"Yes, both." Josie proceeded to do that.

Five minutes later, Tom arrived. "A body?" He approached the women at the table. "In the chill chest?"

"The walk-in."

"Oh, yes. Well. Fresh kill, I take it?"

Annie chuckled once at his levity before recalling the sight of the dead man crumpled in the back corner of the walk-in. "At first, I thought it was a pile of rags. Someone just dumped him in there. Dave thinks he wasn't killed there."

Just then, Dave came out of the kitchen. "I'll go upstairs and check the room, if I may, Josie. Got the key?"

"Yes. Room Two. On the right of the stairs. It's the yellow door. And room three next to it, also on the right, the green door." She looked at Annie. "I painted all the doors a different color. It's meant to help even the inebriated guests find their own room. Seems folks remember colors better than numbers."

"Sure. Makes sense." Annie really didn't know but felt the need to make a comment.

Dave went up the stairs.

Tom sat at the table.

After a few minutes of silence, all three attempted to talk at the same time.

"You go," said Tom, pointing to Josie.

"I think I have to cancel tonight's supper."

Tom nodded. "I'll call Julie. She can put it out on Facebook under town news." Tom dialed, then stood and walked away from the women at the table.

Dave came down the stairs. "Room is completely empty. The bed is made, no luggage, no nothing. I'm not sure, but they may have stripped the room."

"Like in how. There wasn't much in there." Josie stood and aimed for the stairs.

"Now, Josie, don't get all het up. Sit. You can't go up. Let the Staties go up first."

Josie sat back down. "Stripped how?"

Dave answered, as he stood beside the table. "No luggage, no towels, no tissue boxes you like to put in there, no little favors, just the walls and bedding and, you know, the stuff that belongs with the room.

"In which room?"

"Both."

"What in heck do I do now."

Tom finished his call and came back to the table in time to hear her comment. "Now, you sit. You wait. Can you post a sign on the door?"

"I have the list of reservations. I'll call them." Josie went to the desk tucked in the corner of the room, taking her phone.

As Josie made calls, Annie looked up at Tom. She was still shaking from the experience. "I have got to stop finding bodies of dead people."

"At least this one is fresh." He shook his head. "Sorry. That was in bad taste."

Annie grinned at his stab of humor. "I understand. And yes, at least this one is fresh. He was alive yesterday, and he's been kept cool."

In the silence, Josie could be heard talking to people. "You'll hear about it anyways. Someone died here and now it's a crime scene. No supper, I'm afraid. Yes, maybe next week. Talk to you soon." The conversation was repeated half a dozen times, with only slight variations. Josie then returned to the table.

Dave came back from the kitchen. "Not much I can do. I just looked around the kitchen. The State Police don't like locals messing with crime scenes. They'll send the forensic experts to do a thorough job. You need anything?"

Josie shook her head no.

Joe entered. "Hear you have a spot of trouble?"

= = =

Chapter 2

Joe went to Josie and gave her a shoulder hug. He nodded at Annie, then patted Tom on the shoulder.

Tom gave a half smile and waved a hand in Annie's direction. "Annie found him. He's in the cooler."

Joe looked at Josie. "Your new walk-in? How'd he get there? Is that the kill site?"

Dave took a seat and answered. "Probably not. I've called the State Police. As you know, they handle all homicides in Maine. Small towns just don't have the trained personnel or equipment."

"Right. I knew that." Joe nodded. "What's their ETA?"

"I was told it might be an hour. There was a truck roll over in Augusta."

"Again?" Tom stood. "How about I make up a fresh pot of coffee?"

"Oh, I hadn't thought. Yes. Go ahead." Josie went to stand, then sat back down. "You know how."

"Indeed"

Tom did seem familiar with the layout of the dining area and the drip coffee maker, which led Annie to wonder again about the relationship between Tom and Josie. However, when she turned her gaze back to the table, Annie saw a look pass between Joe and Josie which had her wondering about that.

Everyone watched Tom set up the coffee machine and put out cups for the five of them.

Dave leaned back in his chair and dialed. "Hey Chet, I'll be over to Josie's if anyone needs me. Yah, well, some something happened here. Just hold down the fort, for now." He nodded. "Yes. Yes. That's right. No supper here tonight." He put his phone back in his shirt pocket. "Word sure spreads fast in this town."

The coffee maker could be heard in the silent room. When it stopped gurgling, Tom stood and fixed a tray with the carafe, the five cups, and the basket of fixings that were kept near it, along with some spoons and napkins. He brought them to the table.

"Dave, can I bake? I can't just sit here. I was about to give Annie a lesson on scones. Those might go good about now, while we wait. They don't take long to bake, but I'd have to go into the kitchen to bake them."

"I think that might be alright. Just don't go in the cooler and don't move anything."

"Oh, shoot," said Annie. "I never got you that butter."

"Oh, shoot," she echoed. "That's right. So, maybe some muffins, then. I can make them with vegetable oil. And with those guests gone, I won't need the scones, anyways."

Dave nodded. "Just don't' disturb anything in the kitchen. The oven should be fine to use, though."

Annie followed Josie to the side table where various bowls, cups and ingredients were laid out.

"The biggest difference between the various baked good is usually fat."

"Fat," echoed Annie.

"Biscuits use lots of fat, though not as much as pie dough. Muffins use more sugar, less fat. Scones are an almost biscuit."

"I got it."

"We'll do a small batch. That will use two cups of flour for twelve muffins."

"Where's your recipe? Don't you follow a recipe?"

Josie tapped her head. "You make them often enough, you just know. Now, depending on what type of muffin you want, you use different amounts of sugar. If you want them real muffin-y, less sugar, but for soft and cake-y ones, more sugar. We'll split the difference here. So, two cups of flour, three quarters of a cup of sugar."

"Doesn't the type of muffin matter?"

"How do you mean?"

"Like, well, blueberry, or lemon poppy seed?"

"No, the basics will be the same. Now, the type of fat can change, but the proportions will be the same. Vegetable oil, butter, lard, shortening. Melt the solids ones, though. And for two cups flour, one egg. If you want it cakier, you'd use two eggs."

"And more sugar. Wow. It's that simple?"

"Basically, yes."

As Josie was explaining, she was mixing. "You mix the dry ingredients. For each cup of flour, you'd put in one teaspoon of baking powder. If you are using acid things, like buttermilk or lemon, you'd add about one half teaspoon of baking soda."

"What's the difference? Why not just more baking powder."

"It's an acid thing. I'm not sure of the exact science, just that it works." Josie mixed all the dry ingredients. Then she mixed some milk, the egg and the oil in a cup. She then stirred it all together. "Once the wet goes into the dry, you don't want to mix it too much. Just stir enough to get the wet and dry combined."

"That's it?"

"Sure. Let's make this batch apple ones." She took two apples from the fruit bowl on the desk. In just over a minute, she had them peeled, diced and stirred into the batter. "Now we portion these out. Fill the cups about three quarters full, bake at 350°F for fifteen or twenty minutes. Done."

Dave turned to talk to Josie. "Looking forward to that. I haven't had your muffins in a long, long time, Josie."

Annie thought there was an undercurrent in Dave's remark.

Josie looked at her, shrugged and took the muffin tin into the kitchen.

Tom rubbed his hands together. "That will be a treat." He then poured more coffee into his cup. "Anyone else?"

"I need to go," said Joe. "Got court and Judge Clements hates lawyers that are late." He smiled ruefully. "Even if it isn't something more than a review of a custody arrangement." He stood and left.

The four that were still there looked at each other, then around the room, and at their coffee cups.

"Well, this is a fine state of affairs," said Tom, to break the silence. "This was a patron, then?"

"Yes," Josie cleared her throat and repeated it. "Yes. They came in last night. Four young people. Now, one of them is dead. The other three seem to be missing."

The Chilled Corpse   Page 13

"Did you try to phone them?"

"No. If they know what happened, they' might not answer, anyways. I'll let the cops handle that." She then took note that Dave was sitting with them in uniform. "Sorry. I'll let the Staties handle that."

"No offense. I mean, I know what needs to be done. But the State Police hate when someone has been mucking about in a crime scene. They want first dibs."

Annie took a sip of her now tepid coffee and put the cup back down. "Can you explain to me the difference between sheriff, police officer, and state police? Who does what?"

Dave nodded. "Simple yet complicated at times. This gets real complicated when some officers put on more than one uniform, that is working for more than one outfit. Some towns are big enough to have a police force. Many towns don't. Sheriffs are county police who cover towns and in-betweens that are too small or remote to have a police force. Just the basic stuff. We do the same thing as local police: traffic control, domestic disputes, accident reports, thefts, drug monitoring and such. Different states have different protocols. But in Maine, the State Police get called in for higher stakes, such as hostage situations."

Tom jumped in. "And murders, or any violent deaths, and Amber Alerts that aren't resolved quickly."

"And Silver Alerts, too." Dave tapped his now empty cup.

Josie poured him some more coffee.

"Silver Alerts?" Annie pushed her cup forward to get some more, too.

"Yes." Josie nodded. "We had one just last month, when Claire went missing. There was a silver alert. It is issued when a senior goes missing. Usually, it's a case of someone who has dementia."

Tom pointed to his hair. "Silver."

"Oh, silver for the white hair. Silver alert."

A ding was heard. "Oh, got it." Josie headed for the kitchen.

Tom rubbed his hand together in anticipation of muffins.

Dave rubbed his belly. "Been a time since I've had her muffins. Been telling her she should start a bakery."

"I never thought it was worth my time to learn how to cook," said Annie. "There was a bakery on every corner. I could pick up anything I wanted, fresh, anytime."

"You're not in Kansas, anymore," said Tom flippantly. "Well, not New York, anyways."

"I hear you'll be staying," said Dave. "Welcome to Abigale."

"Thanks, I think."

Josie entered the dining area with a cloth covered basket. "No butter, I'm afraid. It's all in the walk-in." She set the basket down on the table.

Tom didn't wait, but reached for a muffin. Dave's hand almost beat him.

"Smells great. I didn't know it was so simple," said Annie. "I'll have to try it on my own."

"Help yourselves," Josie said to the three at the table, two of whom already had a muffin.

The room was quiet as they ate breakfast. The two men ate a second muffin.

Josie stood and started a second carafe of coffee. "They should be here soon."

The Chilled Corpse   Page 15

"Ah," said Tom. "I get it now. You're anxious to impress Jim. You do know he might not be the one to show up."

"First, I don't know what you're talking about." Josie blushed as she said it. "Second, I know it isn't always him to show up, right? There are other Staties?"

"Just teasing. Don't' get your hackles up."

Still prepping the coffee, Josie didn't turn. "What if I had a crush on him in high school. Grow up. I have." Finally finished tinkering, she turned the machine on and returned to the table.

"Sorry," muttered Tom.

Dave pushed his chair back. "Small towns. Love 'em or leave 'em." He stood. "Gotta' use the facilities. That wasn't my first cup of.'"

Shortly after he left the room, State Troopers entered looking official in their smart blue uniforms.

The taller one nodded at them. "Hi Josie, Tom" he shook their hands. Then he introduced himself to Annie. "I'm officer Dennis Knots. This is officer Jim Pike," he said to those Annie. "And you are?"

"Annie Carlton. I just moved here. I found him first." She felt a blush rise up her face. She lost all her words.

Officer Knots nodded at her comment, then turned to Joe, still at the table. "I thought Dave was here?"

"He is." Annie went to stand. "He's in the bathroom. I can show you the dead man."

"Just point," said Officer Pike sharply. "Have you been in where the body is? The walk in, is it?"

Annie answered. "I went as far as the door . I backed out and called Josie."

Josie then also answered. "I went to the door and looked. It was apparent he was dead. I didn't go in. Then we came out here."

"Do I smell fresh baked good," asked Officer Knots.

"Leave it. We don't' have time." Again, Pike was abrupt.

The two state troopers went into the kitchen. They came back out a few minutes later. "Yup. Dead. For sure." Knots smiled warmly at Josie.

Josie was fiddling with her empty cup. "Told you. Geez. What's a girl to do to get cred around here."

"Told you to go get qualified as a trooper." He smiled again and reached into the basket for a muffin.

Pike gave in. "Might as well."

Knots spoke up. "And Josie, can we have coffee with that. We'll need to wait for forensics to arrive."

"Of course you can have coffee. You want it in a cup, or thermos. If I recall, you usually wanted your coffee in your thermos in the mornings."

As Dave entered the room and greeted the two officers, Josie turned to Annie. "He was billeted in this area for a while, and so he stayed at the Inn, for the short duration."]

Annie thought she looked a little red around the gills when she said it, not a true blush, but just a bit embarrassed.

Again, Annie wondered at the background. It seemed everyone knew everyone around here, their past and current conditions included.

The Chilled Corpse   Page 17

"So, Miss Carleton. One month, two bodies. It's called job security for us, but can you keep up the pace?" Knot's lips twitched into an almost smile, taking the sting out of the comment and showing that he was teasing. "Do we have a pattern here?"

After Annie caught on that he was teasing, she laughed. "No. I sure hope not. I'd may have to return to New York, where the death rate by violence is much higher."

"New York, was it. That would explain it." He took a last swig of coffee.

"Oh, leave off, would you." Pike stood and went to the coffeemaker and brought the carafe back to the table. "Anyone else?"

Annie wondered at the friction between the two partners.

"Wonderful muffins, Annie." Knots reached for another.

Just then the door opened. "Ah, finally" The forensic team had arrived. They were clad in white jump suits, booties to hoods, as they entered.

Officer Knots took the lead in the introductions. "Medical Examiner's office , under the able leadership of Seth Green."

Seth pointed to the other white clad person. "This is Nancy. Where is the body?"

Three men pushed back their chairs, but it was Pike that lead the way into the kitchen.

Ten minutes later, they returned to the dining area. Seth was in the lead."Yup, dead. A knife in the heart will do that. But it might not have been what killed him. I'll have to get him on the table to be sure."

Annie felt confused. This was forensics, wasn't it? He spoke as if he were going to do the autopsy. Was he the medical examiner?

Josie leaned over and explained. "Seth likes to see the crime scene when he can. He couldn't decide what he wanted to be when he was in school, so he double majored."

"I hear that, Miss fancy pants. It wasn't that I didn't know what I wanted, so much as I want to be able to see the whole picture, and that includes the crime scene, and a body gives as much clues as the place the crime took place. But in this case, I do believe that the crime didn't take place in your cooler." He turned and spoke softly near his assistant's ear. He turned to those at the table. "We'll tag and bag, then, if you folks don't mind."

Dave nodded.

Josie gave a half smile. "Don't let me stop you. How soon can I use the cooler?"

Annie looked around at the people in the room, people she hadn't known a few weeks before. "That's it? I thought this stuff took hours and hours."

Seth and Nancy went out the door,

They returned a few moments later with a gurney and wheeled it into the kitchen. Dave stood and followed them. Less than five minutes passed and the three came back through the dining area and one was pushing the gurney with the body in a body bag. Seth waved a goodbye and then they were gone.

Just then, the shoulder mike on Pike's uniform beeped. A garbled message was sent to them. He responded immediately and stood. "Gotta' go. Incident in Walmart's parking lot, again."

The Chilled Corpse

Knots also got up. "Again! We should just post an officer there all the time. Dave, guard the scene for us?"

"Will do," replied the sheriff.

"Detectives will be here shortly. They'll go over the crime scene."

Josie stood and then sat. "How many folks will go through here?"

Tom reached out to her and put his hand on her shoulder. "Almost done, Josie." He withdrew his hand.

Josie hung her head.

A few minutes later, two men in business suits walked into the inn.

"Oh, great,'" said Tom under his breath. "The D&D team."

"Josie, Dave, Tom." The taller of the two walked up to the table. He stood over the four of them. He looked right at Annie. "I've been told you found the body?"

Annie nodded.

Officer Dubbs sat first, between Josie and Tom, leaving the last seat for Officer Down.

"We'll record this, if you don't mind." He put a recorder on the table. "Present are Detectives Albert Down and Andrew Dubbs. Also here are Josie Kemp, owner of Josie's Inn where the victim was found, Sheriff Dave Frost, Tom Peters, and Annie." He looked at Annie and waited.

She realized he wanted her last name. "Carlton."

Annie watched the interplay. These were all people who knew each other. She was the outsider.

"Did you know the people who rented the rooms?"

Josie shook her head. "No. I never met them. They booked two weeks out. Usually, I can't book someone in that fast, but I had a cancellation. They booked two rooms for four people. They arrived late-ish, about eight last night, and had food with them. I could smell it. They went to their rooms. I heard running water as they showered and stuff, then nothing until I heard them all leave, well at least some of them, about seven this morning." She shook her head.

"Do your guests usually leave that early?" Officer Dubbs gazing around the room.

"Sometimes. See, usually they book with me because they've planned something in the area. Day trips, hikes, skiing in winter, fishing, hunting in season, stuff like that. They don't come here to just be here."

Dubbs was holding eye contact with Josie. "Did they not ask for breakfast. This is a bed and breakfast?"

Josie broke eye contact, but then looked back at him. "They were going to have scones and muffins tomorrow. Not this morning. They told me not to have breakfast this morning."

Down took up the questions. "And you heard nothing, Josie? No bumps in the night, thuds, screams, shouting?"

"Nothing. Not at all." She looked at him steadfastly.

He nodded once. "So how did a body come to be in your walk-in, and you heard nothing?"

"I guess I'm lucky like that." To fill the silence, she clarified the statement. "To sleep soundly."

The detectives asked them all some few more questions, then went and looked at the place where the body had been found. "We'll be in touch, if we have any more questions. Forensics

The Chilled Corpse

should be here shortly. Dave, do you mind keeping the scene until forensics arrive?"

"I'm not busy right now. I can unless I get called out."

Dave sat back at the table with Annie, Josie and Tom as the detectives left.

= = =

Chapter 3

Annie was eager to go home and be still. The vision of the dead man swirled in her head. Until a few weeks ago, she'd never seen a dead person. Her parents' funeral had not had caskets, as her parents had been cremated before the memorial service. Now, she'd seen two in a very short space of time, but that other, the one in her attic, that had been just the bony remains. Here, in the walk in, that had been a real man.

Half an hour passed. The forensics team came in, two people who did not introduce themselves. "Where was the body. And we've been told to process the kitchen and the bedrooms."

As soon as they arrived, Dave excused himself. "Me, I gotta go. Business, you know." Dave rubbed his belly. "Thanks for the nice muffins. Can I take a couple back for Chet?"

"Sure."

Dave grabbed the last two muffins and wrapped them in a napkin. "Thanks. Have a good day." He then quickly left.

"He'll eat those, too, and Chet will never get any, I'm pretty sure." Josie smiled at the door that Dave had just gone out of.

The pair did their work silently, in the cooler, kitchen and the bedrooms. As quietly as they'd come in and worked, the team left, still in their white Tyvek suits. "Thanks," said one of them, just before going out the door.

As soon as they were gone, Josie stood. "Enough of this. I've had enough coffee to float a boat. They've released the kitchen, and I'll need to give everything a great cleaning. Who's in?"

The Chilled Corpse

Tom paused with his cup halfway to his lips, then arose from his chair. He turned towards the door and took four running steps away. He then halted and turned back with a huge smile on his face. "Just kidding. You can count me in. Just, I'm not much of a cleaner. You'll have to tell me what to do."

Annie took a soft deep breath. "Me, too, I guess." She also stood. "Just tell me what to do."

"Curious that the detectives didn't want to see the upstairs."

Tom replied. "Forensics did. Or does. The boys were busy this morning. That incident in the Walmart parking lot. They didn't say, but that's often a drug deal gone bad, and they probably have a body there, too, and then tons of traumatized witnesses, most of which could just fade away. They know this scene won't be disturbed. They probably are trusting the team."

"Aren't you curious what might have been left behind?"

"No. I don't like to go poking my nose in police business."

It seemed an odd comment to Annie, as if Josie had been in trouble for just such a thing.

"Kitchen will take me all day." Josie sighed.

"Oh, I can't give you all day," said Tom, in a pouting manner.

Annie couldn't help but laugh at his theatrics.

"We'll start in the cooler. Tom, you can help by lugging stuff out. Annie, if you could wipe stuff down as he takes it out. I'll get you a bucket of soapy water and some rags. I'll wipe down inside the cooler and we should then be able to put everything back in short order. I hadn't been planning on a very big weekend."

The trio went to work. After the cooler was empty, wiped down, and reloaded, each person started in a corner and they went around the kitchen, basically just wiping down the surfaces.

Josie stepped back. "There, done. Been meaning to do a spring cleaning."

Tom chortled. "You do know it's fall, right?"

Annie felt a grin spread across her face. "Now, will you go upstairs and check? Will we have to clean that, too?"

Tom looked at Josie. "They did ask that we not touch anything until they can get back here. We can just open the door and lean in, see if anything seems out of place."

Josie nodded and went behind the check-in desk and got a set of keys from a drawer.

The trio went upstairs. "So, that room and that room." She pointed to two of the four doors.

Tom reached for one of the handles. "Do you know who was in which room?"

"No. I handed two keys over and told them which rooms were theirs and didn't check."

Tom turned the handle as Josie stepped up with the keys. "It's open," he said. The door swung in without need of the key.

All three snugged in together in the doorway and peered into the room. The bed was made, a bedside lamp was on, a key rested on a small desk in the room, and everything else looked as if no one had been in the room.

Josie was the first to lean back. "So, is your curiosity satisfied?"

The Chilled Corpse

Annie backed out, too. "Yes. Now, the second room."

Tom led the way. That room wasn't locked either. The key lay on an identical small desk, the bed was made, the room darkening curtains were open,, and there were no lights on in this room. Again, all three crowded shoulder to shoulder in the doorway and leaned in.

"Looks as if no one had been here last night, except for the key on the desk. See anything, Josie?"

"No. Someone knows how to make a bed, though. Or it wasn't slept in. Maybe someone did some housekeeping somewhere."

"Housekeeping?" Annie felt confused.

"Yes, as in motels or hotels. People who work in those places are called housekeeping."

"Oh, yes, I've seen that in movies. It's always the housekeeper, announces '*housekeeping*', unlocks the door, enters, sees a bloody body and screams."

Tom nodded. "I like the scream part. Always so theatric."

"Yes. Theatric. Twice now, I've found bodies, and I didn't scream."

"Good to know." Tom aimed a pretend leer at Annie. "Good to know that about you, that you're not a screamer."

Josie pulled the door closed. "Let's go."

"Great idea. I sure wouldn't want to hire out for housekeeping." Tom smiled to show he was teasing. "Besides, I really need to get going. I have a Zoom meeting coming up in an hour or so."

"Me, too. I mean, me too, I have to go." Annie followed Josie and Tom down the stairs. "Did it seem odd that the rooms were so tidy but one lamp was left on. How dark was it at the hour that they left?"

"It would have been just coming light at that hour, Why?"

"Just, it seemed somehow out of place, that's all." Annie took her purse from the chair where she'd parked it "I'll see you. Keep in touch. Sorry about your supper tonight."

"It's a relief, actually."

Tom paused by the door. "You want to go out to supper tonight? You've been wanting to try that Indian place in the city."

Josie brightened. "Oh, yes. Let's. You?" she looked at Annie.

"No. I think I'll stay in. I've had quite enough excitement for the day."

Annie had trouble settling down to anything. She wandered through the house aimlessly before going outdoors. The yard wasn't as messy as she had thought at first. Tom had been keeping it mowed through the many years of abandonment. She picked up a few stray branches that had come off the trees and wandered around the yard. She had time to wonder how big the property was. She could see the front yard by the lake, of course, but had no idea how far to each side her property went. She'd ask Tom.

Behind her house was a totally different matter. There was an area as big as half a football field that had flowering shrubs and organized beds of flowers that looked mostly like weeds at this time of year. She wanted to clear that, but didn't know anything about gardening.

She walked on, past the beds and into the edge of the bordering woods. Oaks were easy to identify because there were lots of acorns on the ground. The leaf made it plain which trees were maple. There were other trees she didn't know about. There was so much to learn about her present life.

She wandered back down to the shoreline and sat on her favorite rock. After a while, she acknowledged that it was late in the season when the rock felt chilled.

As daylight faded, she went back to the house, wishing she'd gone out to supper with Josie and Tom. Would she have been intruding on a couple's date, she wondered.

The library held secrets she had yet to uncover, but she remembered seeing a few books on flowers and gardening. She spent an hour perusing those before she went to the kitchen to fish around for her supper. Still falling back on city habits, she reached for a can of soup and then put it back.

The idea of baking flitted through her thoughts, but was afraid she'd need to phone Josie for advice. Josie had told her that after you make something often enough, you wouldn't need a recipe. This older cookbook looked like it had been used lots of times for certain recipes.

Who had been the cook in the household? Had they had a maid most of the time? Had her great grandmother been a baker? Her own mother certainly had not done much home cooking.

When Annie settled to watch the news, she saw what the disturbance at the Augusta Walmart had been. An active shooter. One person in critical condition. A hostage situation, and final surrender. It had taken over three hours to resolve the situation. The news report went on to comment on the need to put stronger enforcement in public places like parking lots. This particular event seemed to be about money owed after a sale of illegal drugs.

The body in the cooler didn't make the news. She didn't mind. Maybe tomorrow there would be coverage, maybe not. Not every body that dropped got a moment on the evening news.

The library had a plethora of books and she went there to choose something to occupy her mind during the long evening ahead. The choice of many older romances and mystery series occupied her for a few minutes. Finally, she settled on the first of what was apparently a teen mystery series, The Nancy Drew books. There was a whole line of them on the shelves. She looked at publication dates and chose what seemed to be the first one, a well-worn volume named "The Secret of the Old Clock" published in 1930 with second, third and more volumes in the series. She could imagine her grandmother and her great aunt, as teens settled on a rainy day, reading these.

The book was interesting, and a quick read. Soon, she'd taken down a second volume, put it back, took it down, and then decided to put them in order of publication, using the title pages. Aware that she was delaying the time for bed after the horrors of the day, she finished her self-assigned task.

Surprisingly, Annie slept well that night. The phone woke her.

"Hey there sunshine." Josie's voice sounded forced.

"Hey, yourself. Did you sleep."

"I made darn sure my doors and windows were locked and I even put a chair under the door handle and put some dishes on it, to warn of intruders. After a bit of tossing and turning, I did sleep. I assumed those folks weren't coming back. And you?"

"Fine. I slept fine. Hey, did you ever read any Nancy Drew?"

"Sure. Hasn't every teen girl?"

The Chilled Corpse

"I somehow missed those. What's on your agenda?"

"I truly don't know. I don't have any guests coming in for a week. Then I'll be booked solid all fall for the leaf peepers."

"Leaf peepers?"

"Folks who head out into the country to view the fall foliage."

"Oh, sure. Hey, why not show me some sites? We could go eat somewhere along the coast and have one of those famous seashore dinners."

"Grand idea. And there's this glass place I like to go. It will blow you away. Some of those glass artists are brilliant. I thought I might get a few pieces to put in my front window for show."

"I can be ready in an hour."

"I'll bring breakfast and make it half an hour."

"Oh, you got it. I'll put on the coffee."

The two women spent the day meandering the Maine coast. Josie started them going East, and they went to Pemaquid Point, where there was a fort, a rocky beach, and great slabs of granite, slanted into the sea. Eventually, they went down Route #1, a road following the ocean. They stopped at Moody's Diner for a late lunch and continued to Damariscotta, a cute touristy village with lots of small chic studios. When the shops all seemed to blur and combine, Josie decided it was time to call it a day and return to Abigale before it got to be too late.

Annie had purchased a pair of seagull earrings and an amber necklace. Josie had two glass pie plates in a swirled sunset-colored glass.

At home, Annie went back to the Nancy Drew series. After an hour of reading, she fixed microwave popcorn for her supper and settled in to finish the book. Somewhere near the end, she fell asleep in the Morris chair. When she woke, the night was inky dark and she went to bed. She slept well, dreaming of the shushing ocean.

She woke to a pounding on her front door.

The D&D detectives were standing side by side. "A word, please, if we may?" The leaner Detective Down stepped up and into the house, forcing her to move aside and Detective Dubbs followed.

Annie closed the door. "Coffee, anyone?"

"No," said Dubbs, all business.

"I surely wouldn't mind some," responded Down.

Annie set the pot up and started it. Then she sat. "So what can I do for you?"

"You were the one to find the body, right?" Down was obviously going to take the lead.

"I did." She shivered at the memory.

"Just a few questions. Did you or Miss Kemp touch anything? Anything at all?"

"I opened the cooler to get butter for her scones. I saw a bundle of rags, well, I thought it was a bundle of rags. I walked in about two steps and saw it was a person. I backed out and called for Josie. She came to the door of the cooler and opened it, if I remember. She looked in, backed out. No, that's not right. She also walked in a few feet, then backed out. We closed the door and called the sheriff. Then, we sat and waited. He was there in just a few minutes. He then

The Chilled Corpse Page 31

called you guys. I mean, there was nothing to do. It was obvious from the door that he wasn't alive."

"You didn't go in and try for a pulse, or do resuscitation or anything?"

"No. We didn't. Nor did Dave, the sheriff."

Down seemed irritated. "I know who Dave is. Just no one touched anything in there?"

"No. No one did. I'm sure of that."

Down nodded at Dubbs right after the coffee maker stopped its burble.

"May I get you coffee before you leave?"

"No, thanks," said Dubbs.

Down lifted his hands and dropped them, then shook his head no, rather reluctantly. "Thanks for your time."

"For sure. Have a good day. You can see yourselves out, I take it."

After the two men had left, Annie poured herself a coffee and went for a quick shower. With a toaster pastry and her cup of coffee, she went out by the lake for breakfast.

The loons did not disappoint. Shortly after their hooting call, the family of ducks came by, but the mother seemed to be absent. Had something happened to her? Could the young ducks figure out what to do when it was time to fly south without their mother?

She picked up her phone and called Josie. "Hey, girl. How's it going? I just had some visitors." She finished her last sip of coffee. "Ah, you too." She listened while Josie told of the very short encounter. "I wonder how many ways we have to tell them that we didn't touch anything. Hey, I have a question. What do you know about ducks? I'm asking because the lake ducks seemed to have lost their mother. She's not with them. Should I worry that they'll get lost and not know how to migrate?"

It took only a moment for Josie to reassure Annie that mother ducks went south first to leave the limited food for the full grown but as yet flightless babies, who would soon follow. They were guided by instinct and it usually worked.

The two chatted about the previous night's newscast which had again left out the news of the body at Josie's Inn.

"Any idea what happened, any clue from the D&D detectives?"

"They are pretty tightlipped about it, asking questions, but not answering any."

"Oh, wonder of wonders."

"The town is abuzz with it, though. I've lived here all my life, and still don't understand how news can get around so quickly."

"Understood. In the city, we didn't even know who was living next door, which was in the same building, just a wall apart."

"Why not come in for supper this evening. Tom and Joe will be here."

"If I'm not intruding. I'd love to. Nancy Drew is getting sort of repetitive, I think, as an evening entertainment."

"See you then."

= = =

Chapter 4

Her newly obtained house was in order and required very little care, though maybe a coat of paint in some rooms and a bit of yard work. Maybe she'd do the rooms up in colors like the lakeside, summer greens and fall reds and oranges. She could fix up a room or two downstairs in the winter white after she'd had her first winter here.

Raking. That would be an ongoing thing, she thought, when the leaves started dropping. Did handyman Tom take care of that? It might be fun to pile up the big mounds of colorful leaves

"A job. I need a job." Once outdoors, she wandered through the yard, taking note of things that seemed to be weeds and what seemed to be actual flowers and flowering shrubs. It was difficult, at first, as much of the flowers had gone by this late in the year. "A book on gardening, flower gardening, and a tour from Tom, who must know about this stuff," she said to the empty air. "So much I don't know."

Large parts of the day was used top think about what she'd like to do for work. Did she want a job up in Bangor? Go back to finance? Do books for a store or shop in the city? The little mom and pop stores in Abigale would not need an accountant or bookkeeper. Scrolling on her recently installed internet, internet she now felt back in touch with some of the world. After a while, she found the Maine Unemployment listing run by the Maine Department of Labor. On the site, there were many jobs from near and far, but nothing in Abigale. Many of the listings were in restaurants as servers, food prep or dishwashing. Also a few were for retail, mostly in the big box stores, places she assumed were always posting for help. But the locations of the jobs were in Bangor,

Augusta and even much further in Presque Isle. She'd have to look at a map to see where these locations were.

What did she want to do with her life. Hanging around in this big old mausoleum wasn't going to be good for her mental health. After a certain amount of remodeling, she'd be at loose ends. Better to get a job right off, although money wasn't going to be an issue after she'd been here six months. A part time job might fit the bill, or charity work. Meanwhile, maybe Josie wanted some help, free help, at the Inn.

Her phone rang. "Hey, Josie."

"Hey. Look, the D&D team was back. They came in with a team to process the rooms upstairs again. They had some focused questions about how we cleaned the kitchen and cooler. The suited up clean up team went into the kitchen and black lighted everything."

"What were they looking for. We cleaned."

"I am not sure, but I think they were searching for traces of drugs. I hear fentanyl can be lethal with only a small amount, and that you can absorb it through your skin."

"I thought most deaths from it were from addicts who were using it along with other drugs."

"I could be wrong. In any case, they took a long time upstairs, and when they were done, they suggested a thorough cleaning. I'd already done sheets and pillowcases, and now I'm going to throw in the blankets and pillows."

"Geez, Louise. So you need help scrubbing down the rooms? With a bit of help, it shouldn't take very long."

"Sure. Come on over. I could use the company."

Annie put on her oldest clothes and went into town to assist her newest friend.

The Chilled Corpse

Josie had two buckets and some rags and rubber gloves by the staircase. "We'll do one room, wipe down everything and then the other. I think this is just a bit of extra caution. If they'd found something, they'd have had the techs clean, I think."

"You think they would?"

The next hour passed quickly as the two women wiped down every washable surface and even shampooed the two rugs. As they worked, they spoke about their lives. "

Annie took off her gloves to run the final pass of the rug shampooer. "I always thought I wanted to 'be in finance', but I didn't even really know what that meant. I just had such grand ideas of people who ran the world with their manipulations of money. You know, companies bought and sold, or even stock and bonds. But I found it was mostly boring stuff. Keeping records, micro analyzing data in order to see the trends, stuff like that."

"I never wanted to leave Abigale," said Josie. "I wanted a family, kids, a loving husband. I went to college, thinking I wanted to teach. Maybe art, or music, something to help develop all those young minds. When the economy went on the skids, art was the first thing cut, and music close behind. Besides, I never finished my degree. I got tangled with the wrong person, tramped around the country with him for a while, found he was being fast and free with anyone, including some men, and I made my way home."

"I never hear you mention family."

"I'm related to half the folks in Abigale. My folks, though. They were a piece of work. Old fashioned back-to-the-land hippies."

"Aren't hippies all about peace and love and health and all that?"

"Supposed to be, but my folks developed a liking for drugs."

"I'd heard pot was rampant with hippies."

"Oh, yes, but they went on to the more potent stuff. They sold off everything to fuel their habit. I tried to reason with them. One day, while in my senior year, I got the phone call. They'd been found together in the house they'd built. The deaths were attributed to carbon monoxide, but the feds came poking around."

"I'm sorry. That's harsh."

"It was Tom and Joe that pulled me through. We have a bond that's now hard to explain. Joe's dad was alcoholic and abusive."

"And Tom?"

"He's always been a free spirit. He came from a grand family who expected he would take over the family business. He wanted to do something, anything else." Josie picked up the two buckets and rags in the hallway and headed for the stairs.

Annie took the rug shampooer in one hand and the jug of shampoo in the other. "So I take it they just swapped places?"

"I haven't totally figured it out, but there's even more to the story than meets the eye. Both are insanely happy, though. Joe is a lawyer and took over a moderately successful business which had been in place for many years. Tom is a talented writer, doing what he loves. He doesn't really need the money. His mother came from a wealthy family up in Bangor, old money, and his father made a good living. But he's successful in his writing, too, I think. I'm not sure. He doesn't talk much about that part of his writing." At the bottom of the stairs, she turned to Annie. "Anyways, as unlikely as I would have thought, the three of us are really good friends."

"I wondered if anything was going on between any of you when I first arrived in town."

"It's not like that. I was in a dark place. I don't know the details, but the two had foundered somewhere in college and helped each other find their own ways and were there for me when I came back to town."

"So you bought the Inn. Is it profitable?"

"I actually did buy the Inn. My parents weren't financially stable, but their parents had been and I got a small legacy from my mother's mother. Just enough for this property, but it was in real sad shape. I mean, really sad. It was a true eye sore located in the middle of town as it is The town rallied and helped me bring it up to speed, and then I opened the Inn." The two of them emptied buckets and wrung out rags and put the cleaning supplies away as Josie talked. "It had served as a nursing home, back in the day, when nursing homes meant a place to go to have your child, and it did serve as a foster home for half a dozen kids at a time after that, but it was left abandoned for a while."

"That's a story and a half. Have you any pictures of documents of the past lives of this old place?"

"I do. I have an album. I plan to somehow do a display sometime. Come sit. Coffee?"

"No. I guess I should go. But it sounds like your hometown rallied for you."

"They did. Now, I gladly host the meals every Friday, well most Fridays as a way to repay those that helped me. Some leave a few bucks, a few leave lots, and some leave nothing. I also sell baked goods for different functions, not full catering, just sweets. Winters, I substitute teach. It keeps me afloat and doesn't interfere with things at the Inn."

"From the surface, one wouldn't know that Abigale is such a busy place."

"I love the camaraderie, everyone knowing everyone, for good and bad."

Annie turned from the door and sat at the table with Josie. "In the city, I didn't even know everyone that lived on my floor."

"I know the feeling. Lived it for a short time. I didn't like the city."

"So, tell me, Annie. Have you tried any baking since our lesson?"

"Gosh, I haven't dared."

"Want another lesson? I need to make some cupcakes for the teacher's meeting."

"Teacher's? I thought it was summer."

"It is, but the teachers get together before school starts to outline the school year."

"Oh. And it's about to start?"

"Just before Labor Day."

"Fun. And yes. Maybe while we work, you can suggest some type of work for me. I need to do something. I can't just hang out at the house."

"Heard. Let's get the cupcakes going, then. Hey, I know. I think Julie at the newspaper is looking to hire someone. Would you do all right with part time?"

"What does she need? I guess I'm not fussy."

"Some typing and filing, and also some reporting, like someone to take photos of the school groups, sports and such."

"I've never done much photography, but I can give it a try. Good. I'll go see her after we've done our cupcakes. What flavor?"

"Chocolate, of course." Josie was setting out canisters of flour, sugar and two sticks of butter. "You remember what I said about more fat and more sugar for cakes than for muffins?"

"Yes. How much more?"

"I'll show you. And here's a recipe book. Can you read recipes?"

"I can. I just never learned to follow them much. Tell me what I need to know. It does seem 'strange' like a different language to me."

"Easy. Here. This C means a cup. Most recipes will show a TBLS, TBS or capital T for tablespoon, and TSP, tsp to small t for teaspoon, What you want to watch for is if the fat going in goes in melted, room temperature or cold."

"It seems complicated , but now that you explain it, it seems simple."

The two women worked side by side for fifteen minutes, with Josie showing Annie how to measure and mix. Once the cupcakes were in the oven, they made a ganache type frosting.

"So much fat and sugar." Annie shook her head.

"Yes, well, that's why there are so good."

Soon, the cupcakes were baked, cooled and frosted.

"So, will you try this at home?"

"I might just do that. There are some old cookbooks hanging around. Something has been bothering me, though. Why would your renters leave one light on. The other room looked like it hadn't been slept in. Actually, when we first looked in, neither room looked slept in. Are you sure they spent the night? All four of them?""

"I frankly don't know. And really, we may never know about why that man died. The police don't seem to be bothered by it. They do seem to think they were here under assumed names."

"Didn't they fingerprint the dead guy?"

"I don't know the answer to any of your questions."

"Well, gotta' go. I'll go visit Julie and I'm going to try some of this baking stuff soon."

"See you, then. Friday, if not before. And good luck when you go see Julie."

Annie hadn't any real need to go home, but felt she'd monopolized enough of Josie's time.

One light on and one off bothered her. She wondered, after she left the Inn, if they may have missed something in the room, or if the police might have missed something.

That evening, as Annie reviewed the two rooms, a thought occurred to her. She dialed Josie. "Do you always keep liners in the wastebaskets?"

"Yes. It's an old housekeeping trick. Saves having to scrub the wastebaskets. People put some awful stuff in them sometimes. Also, it is very easy to just pull the bags, replace them and lug all the trash in one fell swoop."

"Well, one of those was missing today, wasn't it."

"Oh. I hadn't taken note of that. Yes. One was missing? I guess maybe I just thought you had pulled it."

"Not me. So, where'd it go? Did they need a plastic bag for something? Or did they put something in it that they didn't want to leave behind?"

There was awe in Josie's voice when she answered. "I purely don't know."

Annie felt a tickle of apprehension. "Why take the wastebasket liner but leave a corpse. If it was assumed names, then if the body had been left elsewhere, no one would have been able to trace him to your inn. It's all very hinky."

"Yes. And the cops don't seem very bothered by any of it. They did due diligence, but I don't think they are very worried about it."

"A dead body, but they give more energy, calling in all the troops to a Walmart altercation. Is that usual?"

"These Walmart parking lot things are getting way too common. I heard it was a drug deal gone bad."

"Might the two be related? How far from Augusta are we?"

Josie took a moment before she answered. "About an hour. Just a little bit further than Bangor."

"I guess we'll never know. Too bad we don't know what was in the wastebasket.""

"In cop shows, they always throw the garbage bag in a dumpster."

= = =

Chapter 5

"Did they throw that bag into your garbage We should check the garbage. Yours, and the other dumpsters. What do you do with your garbage? . I don't even know what you do with it. I don't even know what to do with mine, yet. I've bagged stuff up to this point."

"I have a trash can out back. I put my bags in there and the garbage man picks it up. Usually on Wednesday."

"So today is Monday? Does he pick up all the neighborhood?"

"Mostly. They do dumpsters on Tuesdays and homes on Wednesdays.""

"Oh, oh. I'm on my way. We have to check the dumpsters."

"I'll call Dave. He can come over and help.:"

"Will he?"

"He owes me." There was a pause. "Not like that. He owes me for all the donuts and muffins and coffee and meals for prisoners that I provide."

"Good. I'm coming over. Do you have a great flashlight?"

"Several."

It didn't take Annie long to get to Josie's Inn but it was already dark.

"Hey, there, you."

"Hey."

"I looked through my garbage can after your call. Stinky. When they show people wading through garbage on the shows, they don't often talk about the smell of week-old garbage. Dave said to call him if we find anything. He's probably home drinking beer and working on his old roadster."

"Roadster?"

"An old car that was his grandfather's and he's attempting to fix it up."

"Sounds like fun. At least a past time. I'm almost beginning to understand the love of knitting."

"The bad guys on the programs usually drop something in *nearby* dumpsters so's not to get caught with it. We might find the gun, or something with DNA."

"Gun. There wasn't a gun. It was a knife, and it was left in him. I'll never forget that. How are we even going to know if some random bag came from your place?"

" Dumpsters first. If they just removed the small liner and threw it in, it wouldn't be in a larger black bag. If we don't' find something like that, we'll have to truly dig through it all."

"Oh, joy. Let's go and get to it, then. I had hoped they'd have tossed it in your trash cans."

The women walked to the nearest dumpster and Annie gave Josie a boost up and in.

"Squishy. My gosh. At least I know they didn't throw in a bag from my place. I use black bags, the construction grade, and most of these look green."

"That's good." Annie heard Josie moving bags. "It also will be near the top, right? So we don't have to dig down into the bottom."

"That's true. Nothing here. Let's move on to the one behind the hardware. I'd think that will be less stinky, but it just depends on what people put in, doesn't it."

"Gladly. This one really smells, and you poking around didn't make it better."

The two walked to the alley behind the hardware store.

"Your turn."

"Me? You think I'm going in there?"

"I know you are. It was your idea. I did the one nearest because it was the nearest."

Josie found a couple of empty plastic milk crates and stacked them. "Up you go."

Annie shrugged. "Might as well get it over with." With a little assistance, she climbed up and then into the small dumpster. She moved some of the bags around without opening them. "I see what you mean about squishy. I have trouble keeping my balance in here."

She moved a few more bags further towards the back. "Got it. A small clear bag with tissues that seem to have blood on them. Paper towels, too."

"Give it here. Oh, leave it where you found it. I'll call Dave."

Five minutes later, Dave was at their side. He used his phone to take pictures of the bag in place, both near shots and far shots. He used a long-handled grabber and removed the bag from the dumpster. "Sloppy. Those state boys are always sloppy. But this took place on my turf, so I care."

Josie nodded "Good. So, what's in it? The murder weapon?"

Dave shook his head. "You watch too many shows. No gunshots. And the knife was still in him, if you remember."

Annie felt panicked by the memory. "That's right. I won't ever forget what he looked like."

Josie put an arm around Annie's shoulders. "We do remember, Dave."

"We have paper, towels, tissues and a towel that might have come from your place. I'll take this to the office and' hold it for the state crime lab. You ladies all right? I should have come out when you called. Truth is there was a game on but I'll watch the replay tomorrow. I TVD'd it."

"Good. Great. So, let us know, would you?"

"You'll be the first. Well, maybe the second. It's the staties in charge. I have pics of where this was found."

"Tell them you found it. Keep us out of it, maybe?"

"Sure, I can do that."

Annie could see his half smile by the light of Josie's flashlight.

Dave walked away with the bag.

"That'll be a feather in his cap, that he pulled one over on them guys."

"I'm glad that didn't go to the landfill."

"Landfills these days is only in the movies. Everything goes to recycle facilities, sorted, and sent on to other places to be remade into something else."

"I just never thought. Everything went down a chute in my building. I was never there when they cleaned them."

"That would have made this much harder."

They walked back to Josie's. "Night, then?"

"Night, then." Annie drove home, feeling like she'd done something to help banish the helpless feeling she'd had since she'd discovered the dead man.

The Chilled Corpse

The next day, Josie called at almost noon. "Guess what they found?"

"I don't know. When you say they, you mean Dave?"

"*They* means the state forensics. There were fingerprints on the bag. Nothing popped up. The forensics did get some touch DNA, though. Now they just have to find who it belongs to."

"Touch DNA?"

"Yes. We leave traces on everything we touch, body oils, stuff like that. These days, there's enough DNA in something like that to get results. Now, it's a waiting game. Was the DNA on the bag from the victim? Was it from one of the other three."

"What do you suppose? A falling out among thieves? A hostage? A disgruntled member of the gang?"

"It's too early to tell. I didn't see any sign of any sort of unease or tension when they checked in. How'd your meet with Julie at the paper go?"

"Oh, that. I have a job. If I want it."

"And do you?"

"Yes. I guess I do. It will make me feel a part of the community. I'll be out at the schools taking group photos, sports photos, and any other events in town. Julie will do the write-ups but I need to get the lists of names, stuff like that. And she'll cover the big events, like the Labor Day Parade, Lumber Jack Days in the spring, car crashes or other noteworthy news."

"Good going. It won't be long you'll feel part of our little town."

"My people, my ancestors, did come from here, from what I hear."

"True, that's true. Talk to you later. Got a call coming in."

Annie spent the day setting up her clothes for her new job. She wanted to look professional but not too cityfied. She'd seen some women with skirts on in the town, mostly older women, mostly the office workers, but many wore slacks with a nice blouse. She washed and ironed for most of the day, trying to distract herself, without much success.

The dead guy. Who was he? Why were the cops not able to find out. Fingerprints were a dead giveaway. Was no one reporting a missing person matching his description.

Tom dropped by midafternoon, catching her by the lake with a cup of tea. "Are you all right? Had a rough time?" He sat on an old root.

"Who was that guy. Who were those people? How can someone just go missing in this day and age. Why didn't his buddies take him with them and dump him somewhere?"

"Questions are the life blood of lawyers and law enforcement. I'm neither, but I'm here if you need to talk."

"Two bodies in just a few weeks. I'm not sure I want to live here." She gave Tom a rueful smile.

"Let's talk about the yard. Your lawn is due for a good haircut. Will you hire me to continue to do it or do you want to do it yourself?"

"Can I? I know nothing about mowing except it takes a machine, and I know nothing about any of those."

"City kid. Really. And here I thought you'd grown up in New Joisy." He drew out the middle of the name.

Annie laughed.

Tom laughed with her. "There. Now. Doesn't that feel better. Seriously, you should probably go talk to someone. I know a someone." His face reflected a dark shadow of thought and instantly lightened again. "So how about some lawn mower school. I'll show you how to run it and also how to maintain it"

"Maintain. That sounds serious. Just how much effort is it?"

"Not much. You put in gas. You check the oil. When it doesn't' start, you call someone. You get it serviced every year or two. They sharpen the blades and grease all the lube points. Those are all secret, so you have to have a pro do it." He grinned as he said it.

"Is that all?" She matched his smile, her hands on her hips.

"Then you walk back and forth until all the grass is mowed. A straight line is sometimes hard, but looks better. It also helps you to not miss a patch or strip."

"Fine. Let's go." She stood. Puzzled, she turned to Tom. "Where's the lawnmower?"

"Ah, I see you haven't explored the outbuildings. Any reason," he teased.

"Yeah. There seems to be bodies popping up all around me."

"Sure. I'll go in first, just to be sure there's no bodies, or furry creatures."

"Furry?"

"Squirrels love outbuildings, as do skunks, possums, chipmunks, and racoons."

"Geesh. Anything else I should know?"

"Rabbits love to hide their babies in tall grass. Also deerlings, but you'd see those. And if you see a snake, well, Maine has no poisonous ones. But they do bite."

"Snake bite, but not poisonous. Skunks and rabbits in the grass."

Tom was laughed out loud. "No babies around here at this time of year. You might see a few snakes, but they'll run as soon as they catch site of you."

Annie caught his mood. "Snakes don't run, silly. So lead the way to one of these outbuildings, as you call them."

"He stood and headed to the back of the house. "You have several on the property. One is dedicated as a garage, for your car, like for winter." He pointed through the house. "That's over there." He pointed in the direction they were walking. "Out back here is what used to be a small barn. Here you'll find the lawnmower and snowblower, but the yard usually get's plowed. John from the hardware will do that for you. He does most of the drives in town." They had reached the mini barn. He undid the latch and opened the wide door. "This door is an issue when there's snow, as the snowblower to remove snow lives in here. I always meant to put in a side door that opened in, but haven't' got around to it. If you want, I can do that before this winter."

"I don't know how to run one of those, either."

"We'll start you on the lawnmower and see how you do."

He explained the basics to her, showing her the gas can, funnel, gas cap, oil and oil stick. "Just like a car. Gas and oil. And don't run over things. You can really screw up a mower that way. You can't run over sticks, boards, cars, trucks or motorboats."

The Chilled Corpse   Page 51

"Funny guy. Next summer I want a boat. Maybe just a little rowboat. Of course, I don't know how to run one of those, either."

"Of course not. One thing at a time. Basically, if you have a small outboard motor, it runs pretty much like a lawn mower. And the snowblower is a little more challenging but is basically the same. The difference is that you are out in nasty weather to run that."

"Got it. Straight lines, no sticks or living things."

"That's about it. And call me if you run into problems."

"Will do."

Tom bent and started the mower for her, pulling the cord. It started on the second pull. "There you go. I find it Zen to mow."

"Tom, thanks. I was in a funk. Now I have all new trouble to get into.'

"Gotta' go. Things to do. Don't hesitate to call if you have any needs."

"Have a great day."

Annie mowed for over an hour, back and forth, first one piece of lawn, then another. When she went in, she realized she'd left her phone in the house.

"Hey, Josie. I see you called. Tom showed me the lawnmower stuff."

"I find mowing to be meditative. Of course, I don't have much lawn here."

"I do here. But what if I'd run into trouble while mowing. I'm going to have to tie a string around my neck and hang my phone. Any news?"

"No. Just checking on you."

"I should be checking on you. Are you alright?"

"Of course. I had some baking to do for an Elks meeting. I find keeping occupied when distressed helps you work through it."

"Or helps you down the road of denial."

"Oh, it wasn't that. No. I've seen worse. I was just worried about you."

"I'm fine. And Tom was checking. He assigned me the lawnmowing." Annie laughed in spite of herself, as she realized what Tom had been doing.

"Sure. He used to do it all for the last decade or so, just to keep the place up, you know."

"And he's done a good job. He's going to show me how to run the snowblower, too. And I'm thinking of getting a small boat next year with a small outboard. Whatever that is, but a motor of some sort, it seems."

"Oh, that will be lovely."

"Want to come out for supper?"

"No. I have something going. But another time. Take care." Josie hung up.

Annie fixed a simple supper, a sandwich with baby carrots and raisins for dessert with a cup of ginger tea.

Wandering through her library after her meal, thinking about the people, her family, she tried to picture who had read and probably reread these volumes. She plucked down another Nancy Drew, sat and read for a while, with her unknown family in the back of her mind. She tried to picture her grandmother Louise or great aunt Kelly Marie as a youth sitting in this same room reading. It soothed her ruffled soul and helped her feel centered in this strange place with her strange days.

As she read the book, she could still feel the vibration of the mower in her hands. It was such an unfamiliar time and place for her. Would she ever feel at home in Abigail.

She had to reread a few pages as her mind wandered. She had made some good friends. Josie, Tom, Joe, John and Joane from the hardware store, who had come out to help her 'move in' and hopefully Julie from the newspaper, her new boss.

It would be nice to be employed again, even if part time. How long before this house and town felt like home? Would she set down roots here? Even as she asked herself the question, she knew the answer. Her very essence felt centered here. Now if she could just stop finding dead people.

= = =

Chapter 6

The next day, when Annie woke, she knew fall was on its way. It was very cold in her house. She needed to turn on the old furnace. It must run on oil. She thought she'd seen an oil pipe on the back of the house. The tank must be in the cellar. She hadn't been down there yet, except one quick look around No bodies that she'd seen. Spider webs galore and a slight dampness.

Her apartment had been climate controlled, so she never had to think about the temperature. She slipped on a robe and ran downstairs. She knew where the thermostat was. She turned it up to seventy, which seemed a decent temperature and ran back upstairs. The house was rigged with baseboard heating, which ran around most rooms. She hopped back into bed and waited for the heat to kick in. She heard gurling pipes and a few popping sounds. Was that normal? She waited but heard no gushing water and there was no explosion. After half an hour, she felt the warmth. She got up and got ready to go to work at her new job.

Julie had not told her what hours she'd be working or when to show up. Did Julie work early, or did she work late. Nine. She planned to get to the office at nine. That seemed reasonable.

Julie was already there when Annie arrived. "Hey, there, you. Got a job for you already, if you're up to it. We'll get you settled at your desk over there."

Annie saw a desk that hadn't been there the day before. "Great. And do you have a camera I can use. I don't have any, except the one on my phone."

"Oh course. I have several for you to choose from. I have this small Samsung, but I have the fancier Nikon. It has

The Chilled Corpse   Page 55

focus, way more settings than you'll need, a zoom lens and more. It's what I use when shooting school sports and such. I'll teach you to use it. It's super for close ups and for long shots and group shots." Julie stood and led the way to the new desk. "When I started here, I was using an old Canon and real film, which I developed in the back room. Digital is so way much easier."

"I've seen movies that showed a dark room and developing."

"You can get some really special effects that way, but digital, you can manipulate that , too."

"So, what's the assignment?"

"The high school football team has done well in the last few years. We have a few super players. Practice has already started. I'd like to get in a few shots of the boys. There's a scrimmage this afternoon."

'Scrimmage? I know nothing about football, except you have to get the ball across the finish line."

"You don't' need to know, just get some action shots. A scrimmage is two teams who use each other to practice. Season games are win or lose and the team that wins the most goes on to state finals and well, it's complicated. I'll explain at some other time. I'd especially like something focused on number 79. He's made state all-star for two years and will be a senior this year. We might be looking at a future pro."

"Wow. Number 79 it is, then. How about I start by looking at older newspapers to see what's been done in the past, see what it looks like."

"Also, here's the manual for the two cameras you'll be using. Old newspapers in the back. I only have a year of them, as the others went to the archive building."

"Got it. Speaking of archive, do you know how Claire is?"

Julie looked at her quizzically. "You care? After she locked you in?"

"I think she was not herself that day. How is she now?"

"I heard she's fine. And you? You found another body?"

"Yes. In Josie's cooler. I went in to get butter to make scones."

"Seems you're a magnet for dead people."

"Seems so." Annie sat at her appointed desk, feeling displaced, alien in this unfamiliar work setting and unsettled by the memory of the dead person. She picked up the manual for the simpler camera, the one she'd use this afternoon to get shots of a football scrimmage.

As Annie waded through past editions of the small-town newspaper, she thought about the upcoming editions of this bi-weekly paper. Would the paper do an article on the death of a stranger, and would her name come up as the one who found it. She didn't dare ask Julie. A thought occurred to her, and she picked up her phone.

"Hey, there Josie. How's it going? Something just struck me. We stopped looking in dumpsters after finding the one bag. But might there have been more?"

"Gosh," responded Josie. "Could there have been? Let me think. When I did up those rooms for the guests, I'd left three bags in the bottom and then used a fourth as a liner. I remember because it was the last of the box of bags. I usually just put two in the bottom as spares. What was there when you cleaned."

"There was nothing. There were no bags in the bottom, not in that room. I didn't realize you used liners until we got to the second room which had liners and that one was clean and empty."

"Right."

"Josie, we need to go looking for those other ones. How soon before the garbage pickup?"

"Dumpsters on Wednesday, so until tomorrow."

"Right. Right. What are you doing now?"

"I thought you started your new job today?"

"I do. I mean I did. But I don't have an assignment until this afternoon. Plenty of time to go dumpster diving, And we won't need flashlights."

"I'll bring one anyways. Meet me behind the library. I have an idea."

Julie had been listening. "You have someplace you need to be?"

"Josie and I found some evidence in a dumpster yesterday. The thought occurred to me just now that we should maybe have checked more dumpsters. There was more than one bag missing from her wastebaskets, it seems."

"Go. Bring me back all the juicy details. I meant to interview you about the body anyways."

Annie felt deceived. "Is that why you hired me?"

"No, oh, no." She shook her head. Then she smiled. "I've needed help for some time and was too independent to admit it."

"I'll be back soon. Certainly in time for that football thing. What you call it, as crime age?"

"Scirmmage. And you better be." Julie was smiling as she said it. "Your first assignment and all." Julie turned to her computer and started working the keyboard.

"My first assignment." Annie was already going out the door. "Imagine that. Who could have imagined." She was talking to herself on her way to her car. "Who could have imagined a few weeks ago, that I'd own aa great big old house find two bodies, get locked in a vault, have some really good friends and get a job on a newspaper?"

Josie was waiting for her. "Your idea, in you go."

"The stuff behind a library shouldn't be too nasty, right?"

"Depends what people eat. Depends what goes in."

Annie found the dumpster was almost empty. She slid into it. These bags of garbage were not as full or squishy as in the one behind the hardware. She moved just a of few of the bags. "Got it." She pulled up a small clear plastic bag. This one didn't have bloody detritus. It did have some shell casings.

"Put it back. I'm calling Dave. This looks serious. There were no bullets at the scene."

"If we're right, then there would be one or two others spread around."

"You are right. Let's get Dave to stop the garbage truck until we find them."

"Yes. Please. And maybe we can get someone else to do the dumpster diving?"

"Sure. Maybe Dave will assign Chet, as this now seems to be a thing."

"Good. Great. Can I go back to work, now?"

The Chilled Corpse

"Not a chance, you." She was grinning as she teased. "You're idea, your project. You have to see it through. Besides, too bad you hadn't taken a camera out with you and could get shots for the paper."

"I have my phone. I'll get a few pictures of Dave pulling the evidence out of there."

"He'll be pleased with the publicity."

Josie connected with Dave. "He'll be right along. He says he's called the trash company, and they'll take an early lunch, giving time to get through the few other ones in town."

Five minutes later, Dave pulled up in the squad car. "How you ladies doing today? Got us another clue?"

"We think so. Judging by the look, this one has bullets in it."

"Nothing at the crime scene indicated guns."

"But we were told that maybe my cooler or even my rooms aren't where the man died."

"That's true, for sure." Dave used his long reacher-grabber and pulled the bag out. "Did either of you touch this?"

"I did," admitted Annie, her gaze averted from him.

"That's just for the record, just to eliminate you."

"I got excited, I guess, when we found it. I didn't open it or anything, just put it back."

Dave poked his reacher back into the dumpster and swung it around a bit.

Annie recalled her intent and pulled up her phone and took a few shots of him.

He heard the click. "Young lady, what are you doing?"

"I work at the paper now. I'm getting a few shots of you discovering the evidence."

Dave looked perplexed, then brighter. "Oh, yes. Well, good, then. Carry on. Me, discovering the evidence," he mumbled. "Good. That's a good one." He retracted his tool. "I'll take this back to the office and call the staties. Have you checked any other dumpsters?"

"No. Should we. There's still like one or two of these small bags unaccounted for."

"Yes. But Chet and I will do that. He's on his way over."

"Good. I have lunch to fix for a coach's meeting at my place."

"Ay, yes. Our indubitable football team. Heard they'd started preseason training."

"Yes." Annie felt shy again. "I've been assigned to take pictures this afternoon of their scrimmage." She was proud to have remembered the word and lifted her chin.

"I'll let you know if we find anything. It'll all go to the state lab, of course. they'll see if these shell casing tie to anything."

Annie returned to the office. She nodded at Julie, who was on the phone, so she returned to her perusal of the newspapers. She learned that close ups of people were more prominent than panoramic shots. After a while, she took out the manual for the cameras. The smaller camera would be easier to operate, had a self-focus feature, as well as a grid to help center the image, and an internal adjustment for light. The larger camera had more features which she didn't understand at first, but the manual explained it all. Focus, long shot or near shot, adjustments for sun, shade, inside, and even nighttime, as well as other things and a telephoto lens which could be put on. However, it was digital, and she could

The Chilled Corpse

choose a manual or non-manual mode. She decided to do what Julie had suggested and use the smaller camera to start.

Julie came off the phone after multiple calls. "Any news?"

The comment stymied Annie for a moment. "Oh, news about the 'dumpsters'. I guess some. We did find another bag that we are pretty sure came from Josie's. It had bullets in it."

"Bullets or casings?"

"I don't know the difference. I do think they were the casings, though. Dave called in the state forensics and he and Chet are going to check the other dumpsters around town for more evidence. It will be a feather in his cap, having found something they missed."

"Oh, sure. I don't suppose you got a few shots of him in the dumpster?"

Annie thought about the question for a heartbeat as she'd been the one in the dumpster. "Oh, no. He didn't go in. He had this reacher thingy."

"But did you get shots?"

"I did," Annie said proudly. "They're on my phone."

"Phone photos work." Julie nodded and smiled as if she'd hit a jackpot. "Phone photos are just fine anytime you don't actually have a camera with you. But now that you work here, maybe you should start carrying one. Even mundane things are fodder for the locals. Supper at Josie's, altercation at the bar. Stuff like that."

"We have a bar in Abigale?"

Julie nodded and turned to her work. "You'll find it, all in good time, if you continue to hang out with Josie and Tom."

Louy Castonguay

Annie went out into the parking lot and practiced taking pictures with the camera. She studied the shots she was taking. The camera did not like extreme shots from sunshine into shadows, darkening the shadows into almost complete darkness. She soon found if she shaded the camera, she could take pictures in the sun of things that were in shadow. Taking pictures of things in the sun while in the sun seemed to work fine. Taking pictures of things not in the sun, if she wasn't in the sun with the camera also worked well. It was a sweet little piece of equipment.

No one at the ball field paid her any attention. She took dozens of pictures, being sure to include some closeups of number 79, as suggested. The action shots were a bit difficult and soon she decided to take only pictures of impending motion. Other people were there taking photos with their phones, but one man was on the sidelines taking those action shots.

After a while, she took her eyes off the view finder, thinking she had enough pictures. She looked around. She saw a raised cabin and people with equipment in it. She thought maybe they were recording the game. The spectators, on both sides of the field, were sparse, but enthusiastic. She noticed a score board at the home side of the field and saw it was 12 to 12, but had no idea what the other numbers meant. As she was looking around, she saw the teams were all at one end, so she wandered down the sidelines along with the others that were there. She saw one man kick the football and it went through the goalposts and everyone cheered, and wished she'd gotten a picture of that.

She expected after the score went up on one side, that everyone would line up for more play, but the teams greeted each other, forming a line and shaking hands in order and the

The Chilled Corpse   Page 63

players then left the field and the spectators went to their vehicles. The game was over. Two hours had passed.

Eager to study the photos she'd taken and see which ones she wanted to show Julie, she hurried back to the newspaper office,

Julie had left a note that she had something she needed to do, and to make herself at home.

Now, there was a computer on her desk, a desktop, along with a keyboard and a printer. She touched the mouse and the screen lit up with the Microsoft logo. Some files were in the list of recents. She scrolled and opened one. It was blank. She opened another named bask2 8 23. It was also empty. She opened several others and they were all empty. She deleted a few empty files, rethought what she was doing, restored them and thought to wait to ask Julie. She then opened a new file. She'd get down some of the basics of the game, though she didn't understand it. She could at least list the final score, she knew the names of the two teams and then she could add photos. Julie might be able to fill in any needed information. Annie didn't have the names of the players, not even number 79.

She was hard at work cropping and adjusting photos when Julie returned to the office. "I see you've found your computer."

"Yes. I'm working on the photos. Any advice?"

"Remember that they will be in black and white. We mostly only print in color for the really really important stuff, as that costs a good deal more."

"Got it. Black and white. I'll switch the app to that."

"Have you done much photo editing?"

"A bit, now and then, mostly landscapes."

"People will be different, but the same basics. And you can switch the camera to take them in black and white. It's the nighttime games that are a challenge. I'll take most of those, but I'll show you how."

Julie sat at her desk and made a few phone calls. She was talking softly, and Annie could barely hear her conversation. She thought it was about the start of school and the teachers. She continued her work on the pictures.

Julie startled Annie with a question. "You ready to show me any?" She was standing near Annie and leaned in. "Any of number 79?"

"Yes. Here. And here." Annie brought up the pictures she'd chosen.

"You have a good eye. I'll show you how to get action shots, but you'll need the other camera for that. Good."

Annie scrolled.

"Can you shoot those over to my desk? I'll finalize. You'll find that you'll take dozens of pictures and maybe get one published. You'll get credit for the one that I choose to use. Maybe I'll do a few smaller ones, You did a great job showing the line, but next time, numbers or faces, please."

Annie was proud her first assignment had turned out well.

"Have a great evening, then."

It was past six. "I wonder if the cops found anything in the other dumpsters. Maybe Josie knows. You have a great evening, too."

"I'll talk to you tomorrow about the corpse in the cooler and why you found it and not Josie. Take care."

The Chilled Corpse

As she left the office, Annie realized she was tired, in a way she hadn't been for a few weeks, since coming to Abigale and she carried the tension in her shoulders. A hot shower and a quick supper were in order, then she'd phone Josie.

That's when she remembered she hadn't asked Julie what time she could expect to return to the office in the morning. Nine seemed to work.

= = =

Chapter 7

Annie wasn't a very experienced driver because in New York City, she used mostly taxis, and so she was particular about not using the phone while on the road. However, as soon as she arrived home, she phoned Josie. "Any news?"

"No. those Staties are tight lipped. If they know anything, that is, though I'm not sure they do. They seem to have no identity for the dead man. They got no fingerprints in the room. It was like I rented the room to ghosts. Gene Gent. Sounds like a fictitious name, anyways."

"Well, at least we saved some evidence. But what do you suppose those four were up to that got one of them killed and why store him in your cooler. Do you suppose they meant to come back and get him?"

"I have no idea. Look, I gotta' go. Someone just came in. My phone has been ringing off the hook. It's like everyone wants to be associated with news, good or bad."

"Later, then."

Annie took a shower and ate a light supper and went to the library. She now had a television, but reception was spotty. She didn't dare put in cable until she had a bit more income. She started reading another Nancy Drew mystery and was not able to keep her mind on the story. She picked up her phone, put it down, picked it up and dialed Tom. "Hey, there."

"So, adventure, lady? Are you some sort of black widow?"

"I'm not any kind of widow. Oh, you mean as in mate and kill the mate? Sorry." She chuckled. "No, I never knew either man, sorry to say."

"Just yanking your chain. Any news?"

"We've got a great football team apparently."

The Chilled Corpse

"No, I meant about the dead guy."

"If the cops know anything, they are keeping it quiet. No one seems to know who he was. No fingerprints in the system." She shifted in her chair and changed the phone from one hand to the other.

"That doesn't mean a lot. It just means like he's not a criminal, nor military, nor anything else that requires fingerprints."

Annie thought Tom sounded distracted and brough the conversation to a close. "Right. Will I see you Friday? I hear it will be the usual, roast beef. All the sides, but a fairly special dessert."

"Yes. She'll usually does fix your own sundaes at the end of summer. See you then."

Annie hung up. Two for two. Josie and Tom were both busy. She was on her own, alone. She tried to get back into the story in her book and found she couldn't concentrate. She'd forgotten to ask Tom about the furnace and about fuel. Wandering through her house, downstairs and then upstairs, thinking about the family she hadn't known she had who had also lived here she wondered what secrets might this house tell her if it could talk. A cat. She needed a cat. A dog would be too much effort. Maybe later, she'd get a dog, but for now a cat that could be left in the house all day and didn't need to be walked. She opened her computer and looked for animal shelters. A rescued one would suit her.

The evening wore on. She finished up her tour of the house. Had her aunt Kelly Marie wandered around feeling aimless? How had she kept occupied? Had the women of the house sewn quilts or crocheted or knitted to keep occupied? How about her grandmother, who had left Abigail as a teen? And

Anita, of a much older generation. Surely, she'd some handwork, being of that generation. If they had done any handwork or art, none of it survived. Would any of the journals tell her. She returned to the library and scanned some of them. There was nothing about any creative work. No sewing, no knitting, no art, no writing, except in the journals. There were no comments about gardening, except the occasional mention that the yard keeper had been there and the mown grass smelled sweet.

She went to bed when she realized she was cold. She didn't want to turn up the furnace until she had a chance to discuss it with Tom. She didn't yet know if the building fund would pay for oil, or if she had to pay for it out of her pocket. She didn't even know who delivered it and how to order it. Someone in the household had to have been dealing with all this but there was no mention she'd seen in the journals. Was that part of Todd Cash's role here?

Slowly, Annie warmed up and she slipped into sleep, thinking about those things she wanted to ask various people.

The next day dawned cloudy and cool. Annie hurried to dress and go to work, as the house was still a bit cool. After being out of work for so long due to Covid, the very thought of working warmed her.

Julie was already in the office. She gave Annie a quick smile and a short "Good Morning."

"I didn't know what time you expected me."

"Anytime in the morning is fine." Julie put her head back down to her work. She was examining a picture with a jeweler's loupe.

Annie sat at her desk, wondering what she was expected to be doing. She turned on the computer at her desk and reviewed her pictures from the day before. Studying them could help her improve.

After almost an hour, Julie spoke to her. "How is your crime going along?"

"Crime?" She wrinkled her forehead. "Oh, the dead man. No one seems to know anything. They may not even know who he is. If they do, they aren't saying."

"I have a few sources, and they all say the same thing. I do have to write it up. Death in this small town is, well, not an everyday thing, and a man found in a cooler with a knife in him is very unusual." She stood and came over to Annie's desk. "Tell me, in your own words, what you saw and how you happened to be the one who found him in Josie's cooler. Why not her, for instance."

"She was going to show me how to make scones. I went to the cooler to get butter."

"Butter. She sent you to the cooler. Do you think she was involved? It was her cooler."

"No. She was as surprised as I was."

"The name? Did she know the name?"

"He was the one who signed them all in and paid and said his name was Gene Gent."

"Did you google it?"

"I did. It all came back to genetic sights, something about genetic research, no Gene Gent, just Genetic Genes. That information seemed to come out of England. That's all."

"So, Gene Gent, maybe from England?"

"No, Genetic research out of England is what came up when I input that name."

"So, perhaps a fake name?"

"That's what Josie suggested, but we don't know. It could be a legitimate name. Or it could be made up."

"Law enforcement didn't get anywhere with his fingerprints?"

"If they did, they're not saying. Actually, I think I was told by Dave that they didn't get a hit with his fingerprints, and they didn't find a single one in the rooms. It was like no one was ever there except Josie."

"Give me something. Anything. A description. How was he positioned?"

"I walked into the walk-in. I saw what I thought, at first, was a pile of rags in the corner. He was slumped, his head on his chest, so I was only seeing the top of his head."

"Good. What was he wearing?" She had a notepad in her hand, and she wasn't writing but her pen was poised.

"Ah, jeans, I think, and a faded shirt. Plaid, if I remember."

"Color?"

"Uh, oh, red and black. Only two colors. Faded red and black."

"Hair color, skin color, tattoos?"

"Black hair. White skin, well brown skin, but tanned brown, like someone who'd been outdoors a lot brown. There was just a touch of white hair, in his temples. The rest was deep black."

"Shoes or boots."

"That's the weird thing. He had on some work boots, but they looked brand new. Like the soles of them weren't even dirty."

The Chilled Corpse — Page 71

"You saw the soles of his boots. Good. Anything else?"

"I didn't see any tattoos, but all I could see was his hands."

"Hands can tell a lot. Good. Great memory. I obviously have no photos, but I'll post some stock pictures of our ambulance and make this the lead story for tomorrow's paper. The day before an edition comes out, I can be pretty focused and maybe a little hard to get along with. Don't mind me, please."

"Good to know. I won't take it personally."

Julie relaxed her stance and let her hands down by her side, no longer holding the pen and pad at the ready. "Why don't you go out and get acquainted with the larger camera and also learn a bit more about this town. I wouldn't mind more stock photos of the stores and a few of the nicer homes. Be back here about eight tomorrow. We'll have a paper to sort and distribute. I want it all done by nine, so I can get to the post office with the subscriptions that go out by mail."

"Got it. See you tomorrow, then." Annie was gathering her purse and coat, but Julie was already turned back to her desk and didn't acknowledge her departure.

Annie wandered the small town and took photos of the stores. John and Joanne's hardware store. The small grocery story. She zoomed in on the door plate of the library and took a photo of the hours. She took a picture of the sign for the local bank, and she got another of Peter's Law, Joseph Johnson, Attorney.

Walking the streets of her adopted town, she found the automobile repair shop with a tow truck in the yard and a few automobiles for sale. She walked past the archives building and shivered at her memory of her time locked in the vault. She heard children and walked a little further and found the town grammar school. On the same street, just outside the residential area, a driveway led to a very large building and a sign just off the road labeled it as Shady Acres Senior Housing.

Annie turned around and walked back to town. On her way back, she took pictures of anything that caught her attention, just to get a feel of the camera. She found a crow by the side of the road worrying a fallen pinecone. A beautifully built bird feeder in front of an ornate home was flocked by birds. She wondered who lived there and thought maybe she'd put up a bird feeder, too.

Her little walk had taken up two hours. She returned to the office and spent an hour reviewing all her pictures.

Julie looked up once, then went back to her computer keyboard and mouse. After an hour had passed, she looked up again. "What did you find in our pretty little town?"

"It is pretty. I found the town garage, and the grammar school, and the library."

"What else?"

"I beautiful bird house in front of a gorgeous building."

"Who lives there? Where was it? When did you take the picture? What were the settings on the camera?"

"Gosh, I don't know?"

"As a reporter, it would behoove you to know." She was smiling, a mentor teaching a student. "Take notes. Make notes. Zoom settings, light, place. Time. And most important, names of any people in the picture. At a small paper like this, reporting on local events, names are what will sell our papers."

"Got it. Names, settings, places. Take notes."

"Good. Go home, have a great evening and be back here at 8 AM sharp. We have a paper to put out. They get delivered about 7, and they'll be all labeled. We sort what goes in the mail and what gets delivered to local stores."

Annie stood and gathered her things. "Tomorrow, then."

= = =

Chapter 8

The next morning, Annie leapt out of bed. Soon she was at the office, travel cup and a toaster pastry in hand, ready to sort papers, whatever that meant.

Julie let her into the office. In one corner there were four waist-high stacks of bundled papers. "The printing company puts on labels and bundles them, but we have to sort the bundles. Put all the Abigail zips in the pile over there. Those go out by mail. But watch for the labels that specify a store. We'll deliver those after sorting." She turned to her desk and sat at the computer, leaving Annie to sort the bundles.

"I don't know what's bound for the post office and what we'll deliver," complained Annie.

"You'll get the hang of it. The smaller bundles go to the stores, the rest go to the post office."

Annie worked for almost an hour and hit the bottom of the pile.

"Good. Now, here's a list of the ones we need to deliver. Sorry, I should have come up with this sooner and given it to you. Let's see how you did." Julie went through the pile that Annie had pulled. "Great. Only one stack got by you. Do you know where you put the one going to the Clearwater Video?"

"Oh, that one. Yes. I should have asked. It's at the top of the pile, ah, oh, yes, Here." Annie pulled it up.

"Let's get this all in the van and out to the post office. First there, then these other six places."

The two women worked side by side. At one point, Annie realized some of the ink had come off on her hands. She then saw some had also rubbed off on her clothes and understood why Julie had come to work in an older t-shirt and jeans.

The Chilled Corpse   Page 75

"Soap and water will get it off your hands. It's oil based, and a very good detergent will get it off your clothes."

"Lesson learned. Older clothes on distribution day."

"I sometimes come to work bringing spare clothes if I have to go out in the community after delivery."

"Noted."

In less than an hour, the two were back at the office.

"I have an assignment, if you want it."

"Sure. Whatever."

"John and Joanne are celebrating forty years of owning the store. Could you go over and talk with them, maybe get a few photos in and out of the store. People tend to forget they are there, convenient, close and ready and willing to help."

"I'd love to." She picked up the camera and took a secretarial notepad from her desk. "Be back soon."

"Take the day. Be back tomorrow around nine."

Annie smiled. "Piece of cake. I love John and Joanne."

Julie had her head down and was working as Annie left the office.

At the hardware store, Joanne greeted her. "What you need for that old house."

"I'm here on another matter. Can I talk with you about the store?"

"Ah, Julie must have sent you. You'll have to talk to John, too. It was his father's store and before that, I think it belonged to a bachelor uncle. But I'll be glad to give you some insight."

"Let's start with what you are, a hardware store, right, and what that might mean. In this day of big box stores that carry everything, what can folks expect when they come in the door?"

"That's easy. A hardware store is very focused on those things that you might need for your house, property and garden."

Annie spoke with Joanne for almost an hour when a customer came in and Joanne went to help them. Annie recorded in her note book the incident, explaining that a local store gave laser focused advice particular to a person's needs.

While Joanne was tending to the customer, Annie took photos of the inside of the store, showing the wide range of goods available: cookware, garden tools, plumbing items, electrical things, and a pet section. She had no idea how Julie would choose which ones to use.

John entered as she was taking pictures. "Ah, Annie. Any more corpses. Julie must have sent you to help us celebrate our ownership of the store. Forty years. That's a lifetime."

"Yes. That's yes to lifetime, not to finding more bodies." She was breathless as the memory of the man in the cooler flashed through her mind.

"Any clue who he is?"

"If the state police know anything, they aren't sharing. Apparently, Dave couldn't get a hit on the fingerprints."

"Did he run them through everything?"

"I don't know," Annie whined. "I didn't do the work. You'll have to ask him." Annie felt irritated by a question she had no answer for.

The Chilled Corpse Page 77

"Sorry," said John, in a placating manner. "I didn't mean to wind you up. I was military police back in the day. We had to sometimes do some innovative ways of finding out who someone was. Did they get anything back from the knife?"

"I didn't know anything about dead people when I came here. Isn't a knife a knife?" Annie was near tears.

John put a hand on her shoulder. "I can see you are still a bit unsettled. No, a knife can be a kitchen knife, a butcher knife, a bread knife, a hunting knife, a utility knife, camp knife that does many things, though not everything well, or even a special forces knife."

"What did you do, John," Joanne had come up beside him. "You've got the girl all upset."

"I was asking about the fingerprints and the knife. That's all."

Annie explained to Joanne what they'd been discussing. "Dave says the fingerprints aren't in any database."

Joanne chuckled and shook her head. "There are reasons a man's fingerprints can't be found."

John put a hand on Joanne's shoulder in a way that seemed to be customary. "Sure, and before that we were having a perfectly innocent conversation about how we came to be running the store and have had it for forty years."

Joanne put her hand over John's, still on her shoulder, in a practiced motion.

John took up the well-practiced narrative. "Yes, well. My father's brother opened it in 1920. He and his sister ran it forever. She was the backbone. What you might call transgender, now, what we called a dyke back then. I guess that's offensive, now. She always dressed in man's clothes, knew more about plumbing and electric than anyone, knew the history of all the houses around, was a font of knowledge about gardening, and could fix about any car that existed back in the day before they got all fancy and electronic-ed up. She was a kind and caring person, is what I remember, always willing to lend a hand, and often went into people's homes to help with the needed repair, especially the older folks that maybe couldn't afford a plumber or electrician."

"I'll bet Julie would like to do an article just on how things used to be."

John nodded. "I'll write up something about them when I get a chance and dig out some pictures of them, and of the store as it looked then. I have records dating back to the start. During the Depression, they often had running tabs for folks who were hard against it. A few of those were paid with garden produce or beef and pork. Years later, after the depression was over, all of those floated charges were paid, with one or two exceptions. Back in the day, people were loyal to their local stores and store owners, but the store owners knew their customers personally."

"Sounds like a great story. Maybe we can run a series about this store, the folks who started it and a theme of what things were like in a time gone by."

"You bet, young lady. Get it documented before time forgets what things were like before big box stores, great transportation, and electronic shopping."

Just then another customer came in and John broke off to go to her. "Hey, there Ellie. What's that house need now?"

"I'll tell you John. If I'd known what a disaster that place was. The ones who owned it---" The voices faded as John led her down the electrics' aisle.

The Chilled Corpse   Page 79

"John loved those old folks. When he got out of the military, he had wanted to go into police work, but then we found out I was expecting. We hadn't planned on getting married until we could afford a place, and he had a good job. He rethought his career after he realized that civilian police work and military police work were different."

Annie was glimpsing what made a small town so charming. Most folks in town probably knew the majority of the story she was hearing.

Several more customers had entered, and John was still busy with the first. "Excuse me, will you. Feel free to come back if you have questions."

Annie made a note of the quick and personal service the couple gave anyone who entered.

Back in her car, she reflected on John's comments about the knife. "Why didn't I think to take a photo?" She was still shaken by the image of the man slumped in the cooler but a photo of that wouldn't help with ID. A picture of his face put out on the internet, 'does anyone know this man' as a comment, that might help. But she didn't have that image. His name on the sign in was probably fake. His fingerprints couldn't be found in the US database or military one, either. She pounded the steering wheel once in frustration.

"Well, not my job," she said to herself. She started the car and headed home. She'd sort the story and images tomorrow. Right now, she yearned for the sound of her loons and the lap of water.

= = =

Chapter 9

At home, Annie fixed a bowl of instant soup and crackers and went out by the lake. She sat on her favorite rock and listened for the loons, hoping they hadn't left for the season yet. After a short time, the duck family came by, paddling quietly, seeming to just glide. She felt like them, paddling furiously just below the surface.

"Who said a quiet little town?" She stood and went back in the house, not having heard the loons. Once inside, she felt as restless as she had outside. She decided to do some work in the yard and went out to the back garden and started by pulling all those things that appeared dry and dead.

As Annie worked, she thought about John's mention of the knife. She wished she'd had a picture of the handle of the knife. She'd draw it when she went back in. She could remember the glint of steel between two pieces of wood, and shaped to fit the hand, unlike kitchen knives that were smooth handled, so made designed to be a weapon or at least a tool of some kind. Maybe John could tell from the handle.

After more than an hour in the garden, she looked back over the area she'd been working and realized the ground was almost bare. She spent a few minutes wondering if she'd pulled out anything that should have been left in or left anything that should have been pulled out. She went in and scrolled the internet for gardening books. When she looked up from her intensive search, it was getting dark. Time for supper.

She realized she'd gone outdoors again without her phone when she heard it ring and found it in her purse, which she'd put down in the library. She was going to have to do better at keeping track of it in this large living space.

The Chilled Corpse

"I've been trying to reach you." It was Dave. "I hear you've been out to the hardware and interviewed John and Joanne. Good folks."

"Yes, Julie sent me, because it's been forty years, they've had the store."

"Good, good. Look, the reason I called. I just wanted to tell you we have no leads on the person you found in the cooler."

"John raised a question about the knife. Any chance you got a picture of it?"

"Well, not all of it, but Chet did get some photos with the knife still in the victim."

Overwhelmed with the memory, she forced herself to be calm. "Can I have a copy? I want to run it past John, who seems to know a lot about knives."

"Ph, sure. I should have thought of that. He's a part-time blacksmith or was. I don't know if he still does any, but used to make knives, horseshoes, like for playing horseshoes, the tournament ones, which have to be more exact than the shoeing ones, and he'd make those lead bullets for the black powder rifles, things like that."

"Always learning. So, can I get a copy of the picture?"

"Yes. Definitely, but I'll run it over to him myself, make it official, if that's all right with you."

"That is perfectly fine with me. I just don't know much about knives."

"I'll keep you posted if we learn anything. You settling in all right out there?"

"I'm hardly very far from town. And yes. I'm great. A bit larger than my New York apartment."

"I'll talk to you later."

Annie went to the library and scanned the shelves. One shelf was just paperbacks and they seemed to be science fiction. She took one down that seemed interesting. "By Space Possessed." She thought it would be about the space race in the sixties. What an odd thing that would have seemed to someone from the horse and buggy days from just sixty years before that. Instead, it was a non-fiction about science. Arthur C. Clarke, author of the book, had written some of that science fiction and been an acquaintance of many of the other writers.

Annie read way into the night, learning a lot about science fiction, acknowledging that much of what she took for granted in this world had been science fiction a century before. She glanced at the credits and saw the book had been written after the space race had started. She read about authors writing books with rocket ships and how the authors asked scientists questions about what it would take to lift a rocket ship from the earth into space, before there were rocket ships, or satellites or any of it. How different a world it had been in the early 1900's.

That night, her dream life was filled with people who were imagining the impossible and asking scientist how it could be done. The images of the dream stayed with her as she awakened.

Below all that, there were circling questions about the man in the inn, the impossibility of getting an identity, and why he'd been put there, and how that could be solved. It would be like the writers asking the scientists for specifics. The knife might be a starting point, and John could be the knowledgeable person with the much-needed information.

The Chilled Corpse

Annie turned in her collection of photos of John and Julie and their store. There were shots of them waiting on customers, pretending to be stocking shelves, ringing up a sale, as well as a variety of displays in the store. She felt the collection as a whole was great and gave a sense of what the store was about.

"Great camera work, but I can't use most of it. I'll only have room for one or two pictures. A picture of them together under the outdoor sign, or in front of their window. The ones with other folks in them I can't use at all. We'd need a signed permission to use them. New age, new rules. It used to be that folks would be thrilled to have a picture in the paper, but now, well, it's different." Julie scrolled through the images in the camera. "Oh, here's a great one. This one of them ringing up a customer. You can see the name of the store behind them and if I crop out the customer, you get a feel that the store is dynamic and active."

Annie breathed a sigh of relief. She'd taken dozens of shots, thinking collage, but of course, newspapers didn't work that way.

"Don't worry. You'll get the hang of it. Eventually." Julie smiled as she said the last, then turned to her computer.

Annie was at a loss for what to do next. A bit discouraged, while waiting for Julie to download the pictures she wanted, she thought about John and Joanne, married all this time, working side by side, until the hand on the shoulder was customary. This job might be the shortest-lived job she'd ever held.

The silence was broken by Julie. "Great light on this. You did a decent job."

Annie looked up from the camera. "Say what?"

"You did a decent job on some of the photos, but this one of them at the cash register is probably the best."

"That's good?"

"Of course it is. It will give the readers a reminder that the store is here, and these fine storekeepers are there to wait on them."

"Glad it will work out. I could have gone back and tried again."

"No. No need." Julie turned back to her computer and spoke with her hands on the keyboard. "We often need dozens of shots to get 'the' one. This is especially true with sports. You'll get the hang of it. You have a good eye, Annie."

The click of keys filled the office. Annie scrolled the photos and saw that it was much more a collage than pictures for a newspaper article. But one out of dozens, if it was the one, was better than none. She suddenly had an idea. "Can I take this home. I think I might want to do something with these other shots."

"Sure," answered Julie distractedly. "Help yourself. Actually, I'd like you to keep that camera with you, for those rare situational news stories."

"Got it. If there's nothing else, I'll go home."

"Thanks. Early tomorrow, maybe? Tuesdays and Fridays are distribution days."

"Yes. Old clothes." Smiling because of her plans with the pictures, Annie gathered her things and left the office.

Once back home, she spent time setting up her desk computer. She'd been using her phone and her laptop, but she wanted to copy and print. Once she had everything connected, she checked her printer and then sync'd the camera to her computer. She then scrolled the pictures of the hardware store and of John and Joanne, separately and together, then those photos of the displays, the aisles in the store, the window display from the inside and the outside and started cropping, enhancing, gathering and printing her choices. She carefully cropped out images of anyone but the store owners after Julie's remark about permissions and enhanced other areas.

There was an area with tents, Coleman stoves and lanterns and sleeping bags as well as cooking kits and knives. The knives seemed huge and ugly.

Another area had kitchen equipment: pots, pans, pressure cookers, microwaves and knives. The knives here ranged from tiny paring knives to very large butcher knives. She wondered if Dave would be able to get any information from John about the knife found in the guy in the cooler. She put asking them about that on her list of things to do tomorrow, along with buying poster paper to make a collage for John and Joanne.

That night, her dreams were filled with knives. Paring knives threatening an apple with peeling it while alive and still on the tree, a talking camp knife that was directing someone's hand, maybe her own, how to chop firewood and a hunting knife was trading jobs with a small ax to get out of slashing into the belly of some beast.

Morning came and Annie didn't want to get up. Maybe she'd let Julie do the sorting by herself, call in sick. It was part time, anyways. She almost believed it herself.

A thought occurred to her as she lazed abed. Would the article about John and Joanne run today? The thought spurred her, and she raced to get to work.

The picture of John and Joanne at the cash was front and center, the picture she had taken. Surer of herself than last time, she soon had the stacks sorted and loaded into the company van. A short time later, the two were back at the office when the phone rang.

"It's for you." Julie pointed to the phone on Annie desk and went back to her keyboard, then stopped and watched Annie answer.

"Sure, sure. Yes. I understand. I'm sure. Yes. They do. I will. Thanks."

Julie had been watching her.

"It was Dave. Well, you probably knew that. He talked to John about the knife. There aren't any pictures of the knife blade, but John was pretty sure it was a camp knife. He explained he'd have to see the whole knife to know the maker and the model, but thought it was a generic camp knife, available in most any hardware store."

"That doesn't help any." Julie broke eye contact and returned to her work. With her focus on her keyboard, she spoke to Annie. "There's football practice up at the high school today, after school. Might be a great time to practice getting action shots."

"Will do. Good to know. I'll go."

The click of the keyboard was the only sound for a time. Annie focused on back issues.

Some time passed. "Go already. I've got this." Julie glanced dup at Annie, then went back to her computer.

"Right. See you tomorrow." At home, Annie couldn't decide on what to have for lunch and grabbed a handful of crackers and the camera and went out to her rock. She'd barely settled in when she heard the cry of the loon. She tried her zoom settings, but they weren't great enough to get a good shot of the birds in the middle of the lake.

The ducks came by. They were so funny, their hind ends up in the air as they searched for food on the bottom of the lake. Why did loons dive, and ducks didn't seem able to get below the surface? At least, she'd never seen them go down. She sighed, stood and went into the house.

It was time to change her scruffy clothes to something a tad nicer and go take some photos of football practice.

= = =

Chapter 10

Annie spent a pleasant afternoon taking pictures with a notepad in hand. This sure beat sitting around her flat in the city, or working at finding a job, or moving numbers from one place to another. As she worked, she also thought about solving the issue of the unknown man as she'd seen him. Maybe Josie had seen something she didn't remember seeing. Maybe there was something about the knife that John told Dave.

After more than an hour, she downloaded the photos to her desktop and spent several hours studying them.

She fixed a simple heat-and-serve supper and having used her first Maine unemployment check to connect cable, she decided to watch some television. As she scrolled the menu, she saw an ad for a program that showed swords and knives, called Forged in Fire. She clicked on it and found it was a competition of knife makers who forged different types of metal into knives and swords.

During the next few hours, she learned just how different knives can be from one another, Camp knives, Bowie knives, and also swords. On the wall behind the judges of the competition was a whole array of strange weapons.

When she finally went to bed, her head was buzzing with too much information about something she still knew so little about. That was an avenue best left to those who knew about such things.

By morning, she decided to ask Josie more questions. Taking her camera with her, she went to town.

"Hey, there, news girl. How's it going." Josie was setting out tables for brunch. "The genealogy group is meeting here this morning."

The Chilled Corpse

"Smells divine."

"Scones and donuts is what they ordered, and of course coffee, tea for some and juices. Want some. I have some to spare."

"Oh, yes. Please."

Josie set a few scones and donuts on a plate, poured two cups of coffee from a carafe and set them at a table. "Here. So, you seem worried. What's got you troubled?" She sat with Annie.

"I wonder if there's anything you might remember about that guy!"

"What. Oh, that guy. No, just I saw what you saw."

"No, before that. You said he signed in."

"There were four of them. Two men and two women. They didn't seem all lovey-dovey, you know, and I couldn't make out which woman was with which man. I handed him the keys to both rooms. He took them upstairs with him. In any case, both rooms looked like they hadn't been used."

"Tell me, in detail, what you saw as he signed them in."

"He was about six feet, dark hair, maybe a few grey hair at the temple. I remember that because his hair was so dark, I had thought at first, he had dyed it." She picked up a donut from the plate between them and took a bite before putting it down on her napkin. As she chewed, she looked off at the far wall.

Her attention came back to Annie. "His skin was wrinkly. Not like old-person wrinkle, but like spent lots of time in the sun and got dried out wrinkled. He was lean, not runner lean, exactly, but sort of naturally lean. He had very blue eyes. I also remember that because the dark hair made me think he might be Native American, but they don't usually have blue eyes."

Annie wanted to contradict her, since most Firsts Nations people now had some European ancestry, but she held her words in.

"He had on a plaid shirt. Not the same plaid as the one he was found wearing, it was more colorful. I wonder what happened to that other shirt. Oh, each person carried one little duffle style bag, like a small gym bag. Of course, all of that was gone by morning. He had on a well-worn pair of jeans, maybe the same ones as, you know. Oh, and when he put out his hand to take the keys, I saw a tattoo just above his wrist. It looked like a huge red C. Well sort of. It had a jagged back, like teeth or speed?"

"Can you maybe draw it?"

"Sure. Here." Josie took a napkin and drew what she remembered, a thick circle, like a C, with the back of it all jagged.

"Like someone tried to move it and the paint wasn't dry?"

The two scrolled on their two phones for thirty minutes and didn't find the image.

"I did international sports logos, too." Annie put her phone down on the table.

"I have to finish up prepping for my history hunters. Look, I'll keep searching."

"I will too. It meant something to him. Somewhere there's an image that looks like that. A place, a team, a school, or even a

The Chilled Corpse   Page 91

nation." Annie stood to go. "Have a good day, and enjoy your meeting,"

"I always like this group. Most are older ladies with lots of time, but they've brought in some new young blood. The sleuthing is fun."

"Good. I'll let you know if I find anything." Annie left, feeling restless, and not wanting to go home, but without any place to go. She wandered by the sports field at the school and found there was practice for peewee football. Watching the mini players was fun. She got out and took pictures. She could study those this evening and maybe have some stock photos for when there were games.

The heat of summer was gone but it was a nice day. She sat by the lake for a short spell, still feeling at loose ends.

To use up some energy, she went out behind the house and started trimming some bushy shrubs, hoping she wasn't doing it wrong. She hadn't seen any of these in full bloom, didn't really know what she was doing and just hoped the trimming didn't kill the plant.

As she clipped and pruned, she considered the drawing of the tattoo. Was it a corporate logo or a sports logo? She went in and started scrolling again. Sports logo, sports icons, C logos, C icons, C emblems. After half an hour, she thought she'd found it. The Calgary Flames, a hockey team had a flaming C logo. She picked up her phone. "Hey, Tom. Do you do sports?"

"Sure. What you want? Which sport? You want tickets? It's coming the end of baseball, the start of football and always the other sports."

"If I described a logo as a C with flames, what would you think?"

"Several come to mind. The first is the Montreal Canadians, but they don't have flames, just an H in the middle. Flames? Oh, Maybe the Calgary Flames? I'd have to see what you are thinking of. Why a logo?

"Because Josie remembers a tattoo on the dead man's arm. A C with flames out the back."

"Good catch?"

As she was talking with Tom, she scrolled on her computer. "Got it. I'll send this over to Josie to see if it's what she saw when he checked in. Later." She hung up, and then realized she hadn't thanked him or anything. Geez. She shot him a quick e-mail, not wanting to start up the conversation again, apologizing. It would have been how she ended a call at work, and this felt like work. Then she sent a copy to Josie.

The evening dragged on as she waited to hear back from Josie. She went back to the program about making knives and swords and watched in fascination as they took parts off a skateboard and made knives. She jumped when one of them broke during testing, the broken part just missing the man swinging it.

After that, she turned to a nature show.

Her night was filled with swords that had flames trailing from them as they were swung like a hockey stick.

Sunday mornings, Annie would have usually just laid around, catching up on the news, drinking too much coffee and eating pastries she'd brought in the night before. Here, the pace was so slow she didn't need a relaxing morning chilling out. She also hadn't bought any pastries. She started a pot of coffee while still in her pajamas and pulled out a cookbook. She found a recipe for doughnuts, but that involved frying. The book was old and had only older recipes and scones weren't in it. What else? She discarded one category after another. Pies, pound cake, one bowl gold cake, one bowl silver cake, banana bread, because she had no ripe bananas, and so on. Then she got to the muffin section. Pineapple muffins. She had pineapple tidbits she'd bought to snack on. She could do this.

Staying focused, she carefully laid out all the ingredients in the order they were listed. After reading the directions, turning on the oven and mixing, she spooned out carefully until they all looked even and baked for the prescribed time. She was astounded to find the wet stuff turned into baked stuff and more surprised that the muffins tasted good. She'd done it. She'd baked something decent.

After brunch, she went and sat by the lake. How lovely it would be to have some good chairs and maybe a small table out here. The ducks came by as she waited to hear the loons, reminding her she hadn't done any research on ducks and loons yet. There must be a book or internet article on lake birds. She also needed to find a good book on backyard old-fashioned gardens, so she knew what she was doing, what to expect.

The day dragged by, but she spent it alone and was glad she wouldn't have to return to the workday rush of the city, or the tedious task of trying to find a job. Soon, she'd have enough to live on without any need for any of that. She contemplated what she might do with her life, tried to imagine what the ladies who'd lived here had done with their long days, and sort of understood why the young Kelly Maire had thrown parties. Party. That's what she needed. She'd throw a shindig, as her mom used to call them. Labor Day was fast approaching. She could have an end of summer picnic. If she made it buffet style, it wouldn't be expensive.

Tom and Josie could help her make up a list of people to invite. "Oh, gosh. I'll get a reputation like Kelly Maire," she said to the ducks as they paddled away along the shoreline."

= = =

Chapter 11

After sitting by the water for a while, the rock she was on was feeling hard and she stood and went in. She called Josie first. "Did you get the image? Is that what you saw?"

"I've been busy. I did glance at it. And yes, that was somewhat like I saw."

"That's it, then. I'll call Dave. No one found his fingerprints because he's Canadian."

"Wouldn't someone have run an international search?"

"Geez, I don't know. How would I know?" Annie felt frustrated by how much she didn't know, though she'd always felt well-educated.

"Gotta' go. Got a group coming in the door. It'll be afternoon tea."

"Oh, yes. Later."

Sunday. Would Dave be at the office? Unlikely. She'd wait until tomorrow morning.

She spent time puttering in the library and found a book on gardening, but it was vegetable gardening. She needed to find out about her flowers and shrubs. She went to the computer and poked around on Amazon books. So many books. Did anyone buy real books anymore or just electronic books. She wanted a real book.

Next, she went to eBay and scrolled around for a while. Anything that looked old timey also had a hefty price tag. Flower Gardening for Beginners is what she ordered. I might allow her to get a handle on what was out in the yard and how to take care of plants next growing season. No sooner had she ordered than she got a Facebook ad about a site that identified shrubs from a picture. Plant Snap. Who knew? You take a picture of the plant, and it gets identified.

As she scrolled, she thought about her idea of hosting a picnic in her yard. How did one host a backyard picnic, she wondered. First was a list of people she had gotten to know in Abigail. Josie, Joe, Tom, Julie and Dave, of course. As she put his name on the list, she wondered if she should invite his associates, too. Chet, she remembered, often manned the front desk. She'd met him during their dumpster diving foray.

Maybe she'd just put out a general invitation and see who showed up? Might that be asking for trouble? Could she make it a huge event? Should she? There were only a few weeks. She didn't have tables or chairs for lots of folks. Best keep it simple. She vacillated up and down on the numbers. Maybe next year she would be in a better place to do a huge event. Keep it small, for now.

She hogged down the list from everyone she'd met to the few she had gotten to know a bit better.

With morning came excitement, eager to share what she'd learned about the tattooed logo. Surely Dave would know how to tap into that fingerprint database?

She dialed the sheriff's office at nine, only to find he wasn't in. He'd been called out to a traffic accident. She gave Chet the reason for her call and was reassured Dave would call back.

Maybe something needed doing at the newspaper office, because she needed something to do. This life of leisure could be boring.

Julie greeted her with pleasure. "Look, there's an accident just off the turnpike. Seems like a nasty one. Could you go out and get me a few photos? We'll get the details later. Maybe get a photo of one of the cars, both in the same shot, if possible, and people working at the scene. I want those, but can't leave just now, I'm putting together tomorrow's edition."

"Glad to." Hoping it wouldn't' be a gory event with blood and dead people, she was determined to fulfill her job. Being a photographer for a newspaper felt like something important, something the townspeople would want to read about.

She followed a wrecker the last few miles. At the scene, Annie took photos of both cars. The ambulances were just leaving, two of them, but only one had lights pulsing on top. She snapped an action shot of the wrecker hooking up to one of the cars, which had a smashed front end, a panoramic shot of the two wreckers working on the two cars and of the firemen hosing down the road where something had leaked from one of the cars. There were probably people from Abigail milling about; sheriff's directing traffic, firemen, and others. Julie would probably know the names.

She returned to the office and downloaded the pictures, studied them, chose half a dozen and sent them to Julie's computer.

After ten minutes, Julie looked up. "Great work. Good. This will make the front page, I think. That's Otto's wrecker. This will be like a free ad for him. People tend to forget he's there and just call AAA or something and they send out someone from the city. Otto does have an AAA license, but he doesn't get the assignments."

"Good. Glad I can help." Feeling at loose ends, again, Annie puttered at her computer for a short time, before leaving for home. Would all of her time at the office be paid?"

Part of the afternoon was spent in her garden. Should she have the picnic out here, where most of the blooms were already gone, or by the lake, or maybe in the driveway, where the ground was smoother?

Once again by the lake, she thought of her Grandmother Louise, and wondered how she could have left. That sent her deep into the thoughts about her parents, why they never came here, why they never told her of Kelly Marie and all things Maine. She was so inner focused she didn't hear a car drive in.

She was startled when someone spoke to her.

"Hey, there, you. You weren't answering, so I came out." It was Dave, in his uniform.

"Oh, shoot. I forget to bring my phone out when I come out to the yard."

"Well, it is peaceful out here, for sure. You wanted to talk with me?"

"Yes. Josie remembered something she'd forgotten she'd seen. The man. The one--- You know."

"Yes. What is it?"

"Well, she remembered he had a tattoo on his forearm. It was a red C, sort or, distorted, maybe flames? She only saw it for a second." She paused and took a breath. "We found it. It's the logo for a hockey team, the Canadian hockey team, the Calgary Flames."

"Hmmm. Calgary. Flames. Anything else?"

"No. But that would mean he must have been a Canadian? Wouldn't it?"

The Chilled Corpse

"It wouldn't necessarily mean he's from Canada. And Annie, I know you are new to this place, and don't understand how things are run, but we've been told by State Police, who are in charge, to leave it alone. What you don't know can't hurt you."

"But he deserves to be identified. Aren't you curious?"

"Curious leads to trouble in my job. We've been told, I've been told to tell you to leave it be."

"But Sheriff, what does that mean?" She sighed. "Would your search have included Canada?"

"RCMP is who does Canadian fingerprints. And no, I didn't specifically run them in Canada.

"I don't know what that is. Is it like the FBI?"

"No. It's the Royal Canadian Mounted Police, The Mounties."

"Oh, in those lovely red coats."

"Yes."

"Annie, I'm telling you in the strongest way, leave it alone." The sheriff was practically yelling at her.

Annie felt her stubbornness buck up. "He does deserve to be identified and his killer brought to justice, but I hear you, loud and clear. You want me to back off and leave it alone."

In a softer tone, he repeated himself. "Miss Carlton, leave it be."

"Heard, Sheriff," Annie said, looking away so he wouldn't see the spark of defiance. She had no intention of buckling under the orders of a small-town bully who couldn't do his job.

After the sheriff left, she went into the house, unsettled by the encounter. She wondered who was behind the threat, the orders to back off. In movies, that sort of thing meant the lawmen were on the take of whomever had committed the crime.

She turned on the television for solace and found a cooking show she thought she'd enjoy. It was a Kid's cooking competition. She expected to see them boiling pasta from a box and adding frozen peas. That's not what she saw. Most of the plates they produced were fancy restaurant quality. She watched for hours, mesmerized by these ten- to fourteen-year-olds who cooked better than most people she knew.

Not feeling sleepy, she scrolled on the computer for a while. She hadn't seen the man's face, so looking at the Canuck's team roster wouldn't help, but maybe Josie could see him in the lineup.

Her search included the RCMP, the history, the current work they did and the uniforms. It reminded her that Canada was actually British, though here in the East, she often thought of it as French. Yeah, Quebec. When her eyes got heavy, she looked up and realized it was two AM. Time for bed. Not having to get up meant not having to go to bed. How had other women who lived here coped?

As she readied herself for bed, she realized that tomorrow was Tuesday, delivery day, and she did have to get up early to help. After she set her alarm, sleep came easily.

Julie had been right, and Annie had an easier time sorting the stacks of newspapers. She was better acquainted with her new community and was more familiar with the stores and other locations. Most of the papers went to the post office for home delivery. Time was of the essence and the two women scurried and got the job done on time.

"How did you do this alone?" Annie was puzzled, since the two of them were just on time.

"Oh, well. That. I would usually get some help. Sometimes Tom, sometimes Joe, sometimes my cousin Eddy."

"Oh. Right. Eddy." She had no idea who Eddy was.

After the delivery, they stopped at Josie's and enjoyed a cup of fresh coffee and a doughnut.

Annie showed Josie a picture of the Canuck team.

"I don't know. I don't think so. I didn't see him for long, you know, and I didn't realize I was going to have to remember exactly what he looked like."

They chatted about possible reasons he was left in the cooler, as the three finished their coffee.

"If you gals will excuse me, I have to put together a tray of various sweets for a birthday party at the senior home."

"That large building on the West side of town?"

"Yes. They call it the retirement home, but it's just a cut above a nursing home, sort of assisted living, I think. The Peltier Home."

"I need to get back to work, too. And Annie, could you maybe swing by and get a picture of the front of Peters law practice? He wants a new ad."

"Sure. I can. I'll see you later, then."

= = =

Chapter 12

The rest of the day dragged on. Annie went to the garden and took pictures of some of the shrubs to put through the app to identify them, so she'd know what she was dealing with when she got her book. She then went inside and monkeyed around with the app. After an hour of that, all the names of shrubs blended until she was confused.

She fixed a pasta supper which was a little reminiscent of her mother's casserole, hamburg, cheese soup over pasta and baked. After supper, she went to the lakeside. The air was cooler, and evenings were much shorter then when she first arrived in Abigale such a short time ago. How much her life had changed. She'd thought of herself as a well-educated, city dwelling, office worker who was alone in the world. Now, she was a country dweller and property owner with many friends and a family history she hadn't known about.

Did the man she'd found at Josie's have family who wondered where he was? An employer that was looking for him? Friends, neighbors, possibly a pet? Was he a criminal? How about his companions. Were they the ones that killed him? Did they put him there? Why leave him where he'd be found so quickly?

She went in and started Googling things about Canada. The more she tried to learn, the more she could see she knew nothing.

She finally gave up poking around and watched some television. She found the local public broadcasting stations fascinating. "Finding Your Roots" was a program where the host, along with a large genealogical team, dug up the backgrounds of a person's family. This struck a sharp note for Annie. She hadn't known her own background until very recently.

The Chilled Corpse

After the program, she went back to the computer. She started snooping around for 'missing persons' in Calgary. She found out it was a city of over one million people, located in the province of Alberta, a 'plains' state, like the US mid-west and they had no missing persons roster on the internet.

It was after midnight when she finally closed the computer and went to bed.

In the morning, she decided to go to the city. She'd grocery shop and load up on bath supplies and more. A grand day shopping in what passed for a city would lift her mood.

With her car loaded with the spoils of spending money and her head abuzz with having been around lots of people, she turned towards home. She stopped at Josie's and visited for a few minutes, but Josie was busy. "Just look at the roster for a minute, will you. See if you recognize him. I forgot to show you when I was here."

"I've told you. I didn't see him for long." Josie was abrupt, seeming in a hurry to get back to work.

"They got to you. Someone told you to leave it alone."

She didn't look at Annie as she spoke. "I just don't see any point in beating a dead horse, Annie." Her tone expressed frustration and again she didn't look at Annie.

"They did, didn't they. Was it Dave?"

"No, it wasn't." Realizing she'd tripped up, she looked up at Annie. "It wasn't Dave, and no one has told me to leave it alone. Just, I think we'd be better off to just forget it all."

"Don't you think his folks should know what happened."

"Annie." Josie's voice was sharp. "We don't know what happened, do we. We just know he was found here, and we don't' know how he ended up with a knife in his chest, and we don't know who put him in my cooler. Now, I have supper to prepare. If you don't mind."

"Got it. I'll see myself out, and you have a good day."

Fuming as she made her way home, distracted by her desire to find some clue to the identity of the man, she ripped one of her bags and had to scramble around for her fruit. Finally getting things together, she loaded her arms and headed for the front door, but struggled to get in, had to put some bags down to get the door unlocked.

Immediately, the house felt different. It smelled of pine, or something piney, like pine cleaners or Christmas trees. The odor was faint, and she chalked it off to a change of season. Maybe she'd left a window open. She put her bags down on the kitchen table and went back to the door stoop and brought those bags in and headed for the car for a third armful of bags.

Once back in the kitchen she unloaded her groceries, setting aside the new towels for the downstairs. Once everything was in place, she headed for the library and her computer to continue her search. Maybe some nearby provinces would be more fruitful in her search for missing persons.

When she opened the library door, she gasped. The strong scent of pine hit her first, but what had her stagger back was a man sitting at her desk, looking back at her.

She looked at him for a full minute before she decided to take the situation head on. She was a city girl and didn't back down from strange situations. "Who are you and how'd you get in here." She almost laughed at the sound of the classic movie line. Her heart was beating too fast, though.

"Hello, Annie. My name is Andy. How are you this fine day?"

"Who are you? Leave, at once."

"I've come here with a message for you. You are the one that found a man in the cooler at the Inn, right.?"

Annie reached for her phone in her pocket. She brought it up to take a picture.

"Please don't do that." His voice was gentle and soft, but there was an inherent threat behind the soft words.

"Don't what. Why are you here?"

"I'm here to tell you to please leave the situation alone. There could be serious consequences if you continue your hunt for something that is none of your business."

"And just who are you to tell me that?"

"As I said, my name is Andy. I'm RCMP. We've got everything under control. Just leave it."

Annie continued to stare at him.

"Royal Canadian Mounted Police."

"Let me see some ID."

"I'm currently traveling without ID."

It took her several heartbeats to process what he was saying and the implications. "You are police without ID. Like undercover, then?" She waited until he had a chance to respond. After a moment, she thought of something. "Was *that* man RCMP?"

He responded to her question. "I am not at liberty to give you that information."

"He was, wasn't he?" She stepped forward, feeling braver. "It was some sort of undercover gig, and it went bad, didn't it?"

"Just leave it. You could trigger some things you are not aware of, and it could be dangerous for you or for others if you continue digging around. This isn't the high city. People around here are aware of you, and of what you do."

"Are you threatening me?"

"No. I am explaining to you that this situation might get out of hand. You need to leave it alone."

Annie's city bravado surfaced. "You come in here, in my house, and anyways, how'd you get in here? You barge in and tell me what to do. How dare you. And how do I know you are who you say you are."

"Ah, there's the rub. And furthermore, I need you not to tell anyone I was here. So, for now, anyways, you don't talk about what you found, and you don't go poking your nose into something you don't understand." He stood. "Am I making myself plain."

Annie stepped back. This man was massive and could really hurt her. She palmed her phone, ready to dial 9-1-1.

"Am I clear?"

"Yes. You are telling me that I'm to leave the case alone. I don't investigate who that man was."

"Perfect. Have a good day, then."

He walked right at her, and she stepped aside to let him out the door. She heard him open and close the front door.

She shakily walked to the chair behind the desk where he had recently been sitting. It reeked of pine. Her knees were almost weak and she sat heavily. She momentarily put her head in her hands, elbows planted on the desk.

Her thoughts ran the gamut of calling Josie to tell her of the event, or even Dave to check if he knew anything about the man named Andy. The memory of his stern warning prevented her. How had he known she was probing the internet for more information? Was her computer bugged, or her house? She'd have to be more careful. And as she thought about it, seated here, at her own desk in her own house, the encounter seemed less and less real. Was the man really part of the Mounties? She should have asked where his red coat was or insisted more forcefully on seeing some ID or some sort.

Completely unnerved that someone had entered her house and then waited for her calmly behind a closed door, she abruptly stood and went to check all the windows and doors. None were opened or even unlocked. The house had been secure. He'd broken in, then. She'd never felt the need of a security system, but she sure did now.

> She punched in the number for Tom. She put the phone down before actually dialing. How would she explain her urgent need for a security system? She'd been told not to mention the visit. A line from a very old television show came to her 'Who was that masked man?' Only this one didn't come with a mask, but was still a stranger, a strange man, for sure.= = =

Chapter 13

The evening passed slowly. Her skin felt it might pop off, as she wondered if someone else might enter her house. There was no one around to hear her scream, she wasn't supposed to tell anyone about the visit by the mysterious stranger who claimed to be a Mountie, and she had no way to defend herself. Was that how that man had ended up with a knife in his chest? He had gone into someone's home and gotten knifed?

With her luck if she armed herself with a knife, she'd be the one stuck by it. The sheer size of her visitor bothered her. He had been tall and broad shouldered, though lean of belly and hip. Would he come back? How *had* he gotten in? Her sleep that night was fitful. She needed to talk with someone but was afraid the stranger would hear about it.

As she was pouring a cup of coffee, she heard the loons and ran to the front door. The sun dazzled her foggy brain. They were paddling right by the beach in front of her house. She plainly saw the ringed neck and black beak. One suddenly dove below the water and then the other followed. She knew from experience that they would surface far away. She went back to the kitchen, delighted and lifted by the experience, and took out a toaster pastry for breakfast. As she ate breakfast at the kitchen table, she studied out how to approach the need for a security system with Tom. Could she get him to pop for it out of the operating fund? Would he do it even if she didn't tell of the visitor she'd had?

Determined to distract herself, she thought she'd go talk with Tom, but about something else. He'd have ideas, probably, about her planned picnic, which was still only a thought. She could draw Josie into helping with food, or serve mostly boughten things.

She went to the library and started a list. Potato salad, coleslaw, chips and dip. What else did one need for a picnic? She didn't have a grill and didn't even know how to roast hot dogs and hamburgers if she had one. She vaguely remembered her parents doing it but she'd been too busy in her own world to watch what they were doing, thinking she could learn later. And she still could figure that out, just maybe next summer. Sweets. Had to have sweets. Maybe she could set up a fire ring and toast marshmallows, or even do some smores.

She went out and scouted the yard for a great place to put the fire ring and set up a table. A table. She didn't have a table suitable for outdoors. She went back in and onto her computer and searched for a folding table. They came in various lengths, she found. They also covered a huge price range. She ordered a 'grill table' a metal table, from Bed Bath and Beyond that was on sale for under 50, with free shipping and one week delivery.

With the day now half gone, she fixed a sandwich and went back outdoors. Guests could bring their own chairs. Time to get Tom and maybe Josie aboard with her plans.

Tom was not answering, but his message promised a call back.

Josie also was not answering. Once more Annie wondered if the two were 'a thing', since they were both MIA at the same time. Itching to call Joe to see if he might also have gone missing, she restrained herself.

Maybe she could talk to him about the stranger in her house. Lawyers had to keep confidentiality, after all, didn't they? Or was that just for paying clients? Her head whirled with possibilities.

Waiting for a call back from either Josie or Tom, she fretted. Maybe she shouldn't do a picnic on Labor Day. Maybe this place that was so strange to her had its own scheduled activities for that day like a community picnic or parade or everyone going up to the big city for the day.

This place was an enigma to her and she wondered if she'd ever feel at home. She yearned a little for the city, where she'd known her surroundings, the rhythm of those around her, the pulse of the place. Yet here there was a freedom and beauty that was hard to deny.

The hulking large man who had so stealthily entered her house still occupied a place in her brain, even as she tried to distract herself trying to plan for an event that she had no idea how to put together.

Her phone rang while she was attempting to figure out what to fix for supper.

"Hey, I see you called." Tom was his usual cheerful self. "What can I do for you?"

"I think I need some help planning a picnic for Labor Day."

"Sure. What do you need."

"I don't even know what the norms are for folks here."

"Well. On the Monday itself, lots of folks do their last bit of summer with outdoor stuff. You know, cookouts in the backyard, a woodland hike, biking, even swimming, though the water is typically cold. Those with camps go there for the weekend. That sort of thing."

"I'm thinking of a simple picnic here. Would noon or evening be better?"

"I would think that a later one might be better. Depends who you want to invite."

"I'm think a small some something this year. Maybe bigger next year, when I'll know more folks and have more time to plan. Heck when I actually know what I'm doing."

"I take it you want simple?"

"Yes. I've ordered an outdoor table. But people will need to bring chairs."

"How many?"

"Chairs? One each."

"No, silly. How many people?"

"Oh, small. You, of course, and Josie, and Joe, probably. Maybe Dave, I don't know even if he is married. And his officer, Chet? I'm also thinking John and Joanne."

"I think Joe will be off to see his girlfriend. She lives in Portland. A sort of long-distance thing. I'm free and would love to come. Josie usually does a big to do the night before Labor Day, and then closes on Monday, usually, so she'd probably be able to help. Dave will spend it with his family at camp. Chet also will be off, somewhere, maybe the stock car races. It's what he does. Will there be a campfire and roasted hotdogs and marshmallows. Because if there is, count me in. I'm a sucker for roasted marshmallows." He was chuckling as he said it.

Laughter bubbled up at the image of them around a small campfire roasting hot dogs on a stick and marshmallows. "Yes. I'd say yes. And I don't have a grill or anything and so I hadn't thought of hot dogs or burgers, but I'd really love a hot dog on a stick, I think. Do we get buns with that or just eat them as is?"

"Oh, I think we'd need buns, too. At least some of us would." His voice was laced with laughter.

The joy of such an event Annie lifted Annie's mood. Relaxed, she felt confident about her next question, veiled as it was. "What do you know about the Canadian Police?"

"Regular or Mounted?"

"There's a difference?"

"Oh, yes. The regular police do the usual police thing. The Mounties have been around since about 1860 or 70, maybe. They do the work that our state police do, forensics, stuff like that, organized crime, and also some work that the FBI does here, too. They do fingerprint work and more. What specifically do you want to know."

"I think I want to know if they do undercover work?"

"Some. Why?" The shift in the tone of his voice was a warning. "Is this something connected to the man at Josie's"

"Ah, no. I was just wondering. Everything around here is strange. I thought I saw someone in a vehicle that was like border patrol on the side. Who does that?"

"Oh, they are their own force. Yup. Border patrol man's the borders, but they come to the court houses sometimes for a trial."

"Oh. Border Patrol. Got it. There are days I feel like I'm in a foreign country."

"Understood. I felt that way when I first left home and went to college. So many of my classmates were from the city and though we all spoke English, it was like I didn't even understand what they were saying at first. Different worlds."

Annie decided to end the conversation and not confide in Tom about her mysterious visitor or the desire to install a security system. "Thanks for the talk, Tom. As always, you are a great help."

The Chilled Corpse

"Glad to." He was sounding distracted already. "Later, then."

"Later," she echoed.

"Hot dogs and marshmallows," she said to herself, chuckling at the image of grownups at a campfire. Maybe everyone could sit on the ground.

= = =

Chapter 14

Friday dawned overcast. It made her hope for a nicer day on Labor Day. Could she move the impromptu picnic inside? Something to think about. Except for campfire marshmallows, she could imagine having a buffet sort of meal inside, if need be.

Having a quick bite of breakfast, she hurried off to the newspaper office to help Julie with distribution.

Julie was as upbeat as ever.

Annie was still haunted by memories of the large man who smelled of pine and filled her. The image of the dead man continued to fill her thoughts, though.

Being occupied with sorting and delivering papers took her mind off the crime and she relaxed in the company of Julie.

"What do you think about security cameras?"

"Oh, I have one. I get a bunch of deliveries to the house when I'm not there and I just don't want porch pirates making off with them. As head of the local newspaper, I just like to see who is at the door before opening it, you know? But the system doesn't matter, if someone truly wants in. It's a deterrent. Like urging an intruder to go somewhere else."

"I get that. Should I get a whole security system or do you think a door cam could be enough. I sometimes feel a bit vulnerable, out there in the country, living alone and all."

"Sure. Sure. Well, for me, I find just locked doors and a door cam is enough, for now, anyways. But I live in town, you know. And I have a dog. He's tiny, but has a big dog bark. I leave his leavings on the lawn, too, so anyone would know that a dog lives there. Then, he also acts as an alarm. It's cheaper than an alarm system, and Peaches works during a power outage. Well, I guess most systems might be rigged to, but you know. I like the dog thing."

"I hear you. I should just get a dog. But I know nothing about dogs."

"I could go on about it for a long time. But basically, you need to get one that isn't clingy, can be left alone at home, but is compatible with you. That's the short version."

"I'll certainly think about it."

"Oh, by the way, Joe was happy with the picture of his office that is running in his new ad. And John and Joanne are happy with the article we did about their store."

"Good news."

"This afternoon, could you go out and get a few pictures of the high school. We'll run a story about back to school, along with the bus routes."

"Got it. High school. I'll take a bunch and you can see which you'd like best."

She opted to go to the Inn for lunch, hoping to have word with Josie, but she was busy with the lunch crowd and couldn't talk. After a lunch of soup and sandwich, she couldn't put off returning home. She barely admitted to herself that she was nervous about returning home after the last home invasion by Mr. Pine-smelling, who called himself Andy.

Startled at first, to see a car in her driveway, she soon realized it was Tom's car. He was seated on her rock by the lake.

"Hey, there, you. I wondered if you'd ever come home."

"Hey, there. I'm here. Had some newspaper stuff to do." The sentence imparted a sense of importance.

"Good. That's good." He was looking at her and stood up and came to her as she was walking to the lakeside. "The yard is looking good. You've been trimming shrubs. I've been meaning to get to that. We haven't talked about what you want me to continue doing here and what you want to do yourself."

"Yes. We should talk about that, I guess."

"Let's walk along the shore."

Annie looked at him quizzically but fell into step beside him and they made their way along a path that she hadn't noticed before, which ran past some bushes and along the lakeside. At first it was only wide enough for one of them, so they walked single file, but then it opened up. Soon, they were side by side.

"This is lush and beautiful. I hadn't seen the path."

"It used to be more open. The ladies apparently walked here almost daily."

"Good to know. I need more exercise. In the city, one walks more."

"Yes."

"You came out to talk about groundskeeping?

"No. I came out to talk to you because there was something in your tone when we last spoke that told me you had something you wanted to talk about but didn't know if you could."

"There is?"

Tom stopped at a place where the path was very close to the lake. He guided Annie to a log on the shoreline and they sat, side by side. "So, spill. You know I'm the soul of discretion."

"I guess. How much would it cost to put in a security system?"

"More than you are currently making or very little. Do you have a reason?"

"I just am nervous about living out here all by myself, I guess."

"Cost is about how involved a system you want. You can have just a plain door cam, linked to your phone or computer. Those are not expensive anymore. Or you can do full strategic mode with all the bells and whistles and a link to the local police, which is the sheriff in this town."

"I don't know anything about any of it. Would a door cam be enough? Would it alarm me if, say someone came into the house?"

"Did someone enter? Have you had an intruder."

Annie gasped at the bluntness of the question. "Maybe. I can't say. I'm not supposed to say."

"You did. Was it connected to the murdered man at Josie's?"

"I'm not meant to talk about it."

"Let me guess. Someone came in trying to get more information about what you saw and heard?"

"It wasn't like that. Please, don't tell anyone I spoke of it. Someone was there, claiming to be RCMP. He told me to leave it alone. He didn't show me any ID, though, and I wasn't to tell anyone he'd been here."

"That must have been scary." He put a hand on her shoulder. "Look, I don't know anything about any of this, but it does sound like you need some sort of security. I hadn't thought about you being all alone out here. You aren't very far from town, but far enough to be a bit isolated. Why not leave it to me." He removed his hand from her shoulder and looked out at the lake. "We'll start with a door cam, front and back, which should show most of your yard. And it won't cost much. I'll take it out of the caretaking account. It will be a modernizing expense."

Annie attempted a smile. "You can't say anything to anyone. I don't even know if he planted bugs in my house to keep track, or if they are tracking my phone or anything. Somehow, they knew I'd been searching the internet for missing person in Canada."

"I hear you. Look, I'll borrow some devices from someone I know, pretending I need the info for one of my books, and I'll check your house. Also, I'll check your computer for any trackers. I don't know enough about phones to check that. Has it been out of your hands for any length of time?"

"No, but I see on shows all the time how easy it is to clone or download stuff."

"That's for sure. People think of their private stuff as private, but it isn't." He patted her knee. "I'll get you as secure as possible. But on the off chance that you are being watched, I'd lay off any investigating. Now, was there an open threat?"

"No. It was subtle. Like, if you continue, you might get into trouble or get others into bad situations."

"Like that. Skirting the edge. I'll get tucked into getting you set up. And you say he was in the house when you got home?"

"Yes."

"Those old locks are simple to manipulate. I'll get them changed out in the next day or two. I think I can get John to come out and do it. He does locksmithing on the side."

The Chilled Corpse

"Wonderful. I'd feel better, knowing someone would at least have to work to get in."

"I'd feel better about that, too."

"Funny how I feel more vulnerable here, in this beautiful place, with fewer people, less crime and nothing much for anyone to come after me for."

"Funny how that works, isn't it. Having lived in the city, though, I know the feeling. You are more anonymous in the city, with a sense of just blending in. Like a bird in a flock."

"I thank you."

"Do you want a place for the night." He turned and faced her. "Would you feel safer somewhere else until we get things set up?"

"I don't think he'll be back. This Andy fella'. And I don't think there's any immediate danger. It's not something I'm worried about." She hoped Tom wouldn't see the lie.

He looked at her for a full minute, as if assessing her comment. "Got it. We'll have you secure soon." He stared off at the lake for a few moments. Just then, the loons called from across the lake. "Put me on speed dial and keep your phone near, until we get this sorted out. With the ladies, there was no need. Everyone knew who Mr. Weeks was, and of course his man Todd was around, and later, Kelly Marie was never alone. I do believe you are the first to live here alone."

"Great. Well. I guess that's supposed to make me feel better." She was looking at Tom and grinning as she said it.

"Well, maybe?" Tom was also grinning. "Look, I have to get back. But I'll get started. I'll call John to have him come out and get more secure locks on your doors and windows, too."

"That's real good." Annie stood. "It's been a fine walk. I feel better just knowing something will get done."

"It will give John some much needed work, too."

"Glad to hear it."

The pair went back the way they had come, up the path to the house. "You coming to Josie's for her Friday buffet?"

"No. I don't think so. I ate there this noon." Annie felt calmer now that someone knew about her experience. She waved goodbye to Tom as he left. However, as she entered the house, she found she was sniffing for pine and she checked the library on her way to the kitchen. It was empty and she detected no smell of pine.

= = =

Chapter 15

Saturday, Annie awoke feeling hung over after a very restless night and sprinted for the coffee maker and got that brewing before getting dressed and ready for the day. After breakfast and two cups of coffee, she went into the sunlit yard and found there was a high wind blowing the lake up into whitecaps.

The wind-whipped water made her wonder how the loons and young ducks fared on such a day. She walked to the water's edge and saw a sudsy deposit on the beach. What caused soap bubbles to form. She played in the foam for a few minutes. It wasn't soapy bubbles, but one more thing she knew nothing about.

As she poked at the foam with her stick, she thought about the huge swerve her life had taken. She had been desperately seeking work and now wouldn't ever have to work. Now she owned a house with rooms almost as large as her 500 square foot apartment. She had barely known her neighbors and only slightly known her co-workers, and now she had half a dozen fast friends who would drop everything to help her. The list included Tom, of course, but Josie was there, and Joe, and John and Joanne and Julie from the paper. Others in the community had come out to help her get moved in, strangers, people who didn't' know her at all. At the top of that list was Dave, the sheriff, Mark the coroner. She chuckled at the thought that he figured into her life because she'd found two bodies.

The giggly feeling was followed by an overwhelming sadness at the loss of life.

She had also met Claire the town records keeper who'd locked her in the archives room, and the accountant Marc whose wife ran an antique store, and the detectives from the state police. She still was a bit foggy about the differentiation of the police in Maine: sheriff, police officer, state police and now, the Royal Canadian Mounted Police. A flash of the white car with green logo of border patrol flashed across her memory, which reminded her how close to Canada this place was.

That memory brought up the recollection of a piney scent. Andy had been handsome. She wondered if she'd ever see him again, and sort of hoped she would not.

It was sunny but the high winds caused the air to feel chilly and she knew summer was almost over.

As she wandered the yard, she thought some more about where to set up the picnic. Maybe she'd see how the weather was. If it was going to be this breezy, maybe the backyard would be better, away from the lake. If it was calm and beautiful, a setup by the lake could be lovely.

In the back garden, her brain was working on envisioning her first ever outdoor event at her new home and she was smiling.

There was some firewood in the shed attached to the back of the house. That would make a fine campfire. Maybe Tom could help with that. Did she have to have a fireplace? A fire ring? Rocks in a ring? She hadn't seen anything like that anywhere. She roamed her backyard, touching shrubs, wondering what this would all look like in the spring and summer.

She dreamed of lazing out here next summer and felt an attachment to this place she'd only known for such a short time.

The Chilled Corpse

Her phone rang. When she answered the phone there was an open line, but dead air. She waited for the beep that told her this was a robo call, but it never came. Then a click told her that the person calling had hung up.

Back in the house, she started making a written list of what she wanted to serve at her 'picnic'. Josie went on the list first, and then dessert went next to that. Hot dogs and rolls, condiments, chopped onions, marshmallows. She got lost in daydreaming about one time her folks had taken her to a picnic place that had charcoal grills on a pole next to all the picnic tables. She recalled that her mother had laughed hysterically that day at her father's antics. It had always been that, just the three of them.

She was sitting in the library and scanned the room dreamily. This had been here all that time, a dream room, full of books, gathered before there was an internet to answer questions.

Naturally introverted, she'd not missed having brothers and sisters and never questioned not having relatives, aunts, uncles, grandparents or cousins.

Her phone startled her out of trance. Again, she got dead air. She returned to her list. Salad. Maybe she'd buy a Ceasar, and a potato salad. She'd need paper plates and plastic spoons and forks, too. And drinking cups. She could envision having such gatherings monthly. Maybe she could have a Christmas party. That had her think about what things were possible here, which made her miss having near or extended family.

The phone rang again. Every fifteen minutes for the rest of the day, her phone rang. She finally walked away from it to prepare supper. She'd let it ring and would give call backs to anyone that cared to leave a message. Her thoughts of course went to the warning from Andy the RCMP.

Sunday morning, the wind had died down. She went to the beach with her morning coffee and a toast. As she sat quietly, the ducks came swimming by. They had gotten used to her and she spoke to them gently, knowing they didn't understand. "Hey, little guys. You're almost all grown, aren't you? Do you miss your mommy? I sure miss mine." She was almost in tears as she said it, feeling a sudden yearning to talk to her mother. "Will you guys stick together? Brothers and sisters for all time? Will you come back to this lake next year?" She imagined lots of years of sitting here talking to the ducks. She wondered if she was doomed to always be single, like Kelly Marie. Was this a house of single women? "Well, take care, duckies."

At least today, her phone wasn't ringing endlessly to no purpose.

List in hand, she headed to the city for a shopping trip. Once in the car, she dialed Josie.

"Can't talk now. Got a Sunday brunch group coming in."

"Any suggestions for my picnic, like maybe something I've forgotten?"

"No. I don't. Hot dogs, hamburgers, potato salad."

"Can I ask you to bring some sort of dessert?"

"Are you doing S'mores?"

"Yes."

"No need then. Just hot dogs, salad and S'mores. And drinks. Soda, or lemonade. Some punch, maybe. Look, gotta' go."

"Thanks. And thanks for your friendship." Annie was choking up again. Even though she felt Josie was a good friend, she realized she knew nothing about her.

The Chilled Corpse

Her shopping in the city went on longer than she'd planned and she stopped for lunch at a small restaurant. The selection was meat based. Arby's. Sliced dipped beef seemed the main offering and she chose that, along with curly fries and a shake. Arriving home, she saw a vehicle in her yard and her heart rate bumped up. After parking next to it, she saw her front door was open. She took up her phone and was about to dial the sheriff when John came to the doorway and waved.

Putting her phone back in her purse, she spoke to him. "John, you about scared me to death."

"Sorry. I tried to get ahold of you. Tom asked me to change out the locks." He waved a screwdriver as he spoke.

Annie took bags out of the car and approached the house.

"Hey, can I keep these old locks? I think the wife might want to sell them online."

"Sure, I have no use for them."

"Need help?"

"No. How'd you get in?"

"Oh, that. Old locksmith trick. I picked the lock." He waved his screwdriver again and smiled ruefully. "Sorry. I knew where the spare key is kept. It's been there like forever."

"Spare key. I wonder if that's how---." She stopped short when she realized she'd almost said Andy's name and what he'd done and said.

"How what?" He stood aside to let her in. "Almost done here. I started at the back."

"Spare key? Where might that be?"

"It's been on a small nail hidden in the fretwork which holds up the awning. Put it there myself as Kelly Marie kept locking herself out."

Annie shrugged, her hands loaded with bags.

John examined her. "You want me to move it? Maybe we need a new hiding place. Half the town knows where it is. And you'll have all new keys, anyways."

"Yes. Let's figure a new place." Annie continued into the house to the kitchen with her purchases. She then strolled past John to the car again for the rest of her groceries.

"Got you a real neat system here. And both doors will work on the same key."

Annie delivered the rest of her packages to the kitchen and returned to where John was working. "How is Joanne?"

"She's holding down the fort until I get this done. We'll put in security tomorrow, if that's all right. I have to go to the city to pick up what I think you need."

"Good."

The two chatted a few more minutes before Annie returned to the kitchen.

As she was almost finished, the phone rang.

"Remember our agreement?" It was Andy.

"Yes." Here breath had whooshed out at the sound of his voice. "Stop calling. I remember. You don't need to remind me."

"Sorry if I scared you. I see you are putting in new locks. Great idea. You never know who might come to call."

It unnerved her that he was around, but not visible.

= = =

Chapter 16

On Monday, despite the unsettled weekend, Annie turned up for work. Julie greeted her absentmindedly and put her head back down to work.

"Can I help? Type up anything? Get some photos for you."

"No. One of these days I'll train you to write for papers. I'm busy, now though. It was a big weekend." She put her hands back on the keyboard and typed.

"Need any pictures?"

"No. I have all I need." She didn't even pause.

"All right. I'll just study back issues for a bit." Annie felt useless, but she didn't want to return home, afraid of another visit from Andy. A thought occurred to her, and she opened her work computer. If her home computer was being monitored, she'd use the one at work to sleuth.

She typed in Gene Gent, again. Again, she came up with genetic information. She went searching for missing persons from Ontario and then all of Canada. The missing persons were women or teens. So many missing persons. Where did they all go? Were they running from abusive situations? Had they been abducted, murdered?

Down the rabbit hole of missing persons she went. She spent over an hour researching articles about missing people, abused spouses, run away teens and children, sex traffic, and war victims . So many missing. She hunted and saw no follow-up on most of them. If they were ever found, the media didn't mention it.

Finally, she closed the computer. "I'm going home, if you have nothing for me."

"Tomorrow, then?"

The Chilled Corpse

"Yes. Old clothes. I remember."

Julie glanced up at her and then went back to work.

At home, she found John working on her doors frame. "I've got a new spot for your outside key."

"Do tell." She walked up to the door. "I've never thought to leave a key outdoors."

"You'd be surprised at how many calls I get from folks that are locked out. Should have one for your car, too." He answered her silent question. "In case you lose your key, or the car door locks with the key inside."

"Where on a car would you hide a key?"

"I'll show you. Soon's I finish this."

He was attaching a watch-sized white orb on the door frame. "This is wireless. It will feed to your computer and your phone, if you want. I'll show you. And you have a manual, too. It runs on a watch battery, which is tough, long lasting, weather resistant and easily replaced. I'd keep some batteries on hand, though. The app will tell you if the camera goes out for any reason or if the battery gets low. When you get the notice, don't wait. It goes fast at that point. Joanne and I have the same system. I chose it for ease of use."

"Great. And I have one on the back door, too?"

He nodded. "Later, we can put some in on the side of the building as well. You get some great wildlife shots this way."

"I hadn't thought of that. There is so much I don't know. I don't know what digs in my yard, or makes small holes under the edge of my bushes, or when the ducks leave or the loons."

"The wife and I have a few books we can lend you on back yard wildlife, if you want." He paused to observe her reaction.

"I'd love that. Seems I'll be here a while."

"We had hoped you'd stay. Time this old house had someone living here."

"Tom did a grand job of keeping up the property."

"Yes. He always was a worker that one." He put his screwdriver back in his tool belt. "There. That's the last of it. Let's get you hooked up."

"Let's go in. It's a bit cool out here. I guess summer is over. In New York, we'd still be in shirt sleeves and shorts."

"Yes, well. Especially out here in the country."

The two went into the library. John helped her connect her computer and phone to the door cam.

"John, I'm going to have a Labor Day picnic here, in the evening, I think. Are you two interested?"

"I'll have to check. But I think so. The ladies used to always have holiday celebrations, but I don't think us tradesmen were ever invited."

"I heard they'd had lots of parties."

"Some were wild, is what I heard, way back. But it was for out-of-towners. Not the locals."

"I'm going to do things for and with the *locals*, I hope. Come out about five, I think. We'll have hot dogs, salads and S'mores'"

"Love S'mores. Can't eat many cause of diabetes. Runs in the family. And Joanne has pre-diabetes. We're doing the Mediterranean diet. Lots of veg and fruit. Look forward to a

The Chilled Corpse

cheat, though." He turned to go. "I'll see myself out." Under his breath, he muttered. "Love them S'mores."

The house seemed very quiet after he left. The city was never quiet. Annie was startled by a loud noise. It took a second for her to realize it was coming from her computer which was tied to the door cam. She gazed at the computer for a moment.

The sound was that of car tires on the gravel drive. Her heart beating double time, she recalled her computer search of disappeared Canadian persons. As she watched the camera, she breathed again. It was only Tom. The noise of his tires on the drive had been loud. She hadn't expected that.

As she waited for him to ring her doorbell, she noticed lots of background noises, mostly bird calls in the trees.

She heard Tom knocking at the door and waited for him to walk in like he usually did. After a moment, and watching him try the door and then stand quietly, she realized John had locked it when he left. She'd have to get reaccustomed to locking doors, she thought, as she went to let him in.

"I see John has been out. Shiny new locks and a door cam, too." He followed her to the library. "Is it a good system.?"

"It's great. Louder than I'd expected. I could hear your tires on the drive.:"

"Good. Great. Anything you need done around here, now that your door is secure, and you are staying a while?"

"Yes, I'm staying, I guess. There's nothing for me in the city. Here, I have job, a house, a home." She paused, smiled at him, and continued. "And great friends. Yes, I'll stay. How did my Grammie never come here, or if she did, she never brought my mother, that I know of."

"Adoptions can be hard. I'm personally glad the whole attitude on that has changed, now. Open adoptions. The kids get to know they were adopted and, in many cases, who their parents were."

"Yup. John is talking about setting me up with cams on the sides of the house, too."

"That's good. The picnic on Labor Day. How about I bring out a bucket of ice and some beer?"

"I suppose. I hadn't thought. I was just going to get soft drinks. The whole alcohol thing confuses me. I don't drink much and don't 'know a whole lot about what others like."

"Beer will be fine, along with soft drinks for those that don't drink."

"That will be great, then. I haven't decided if I want 'out by the lake' or 'in the back garden'."

"Lakeside would be cool. As in cold breeze." He nodded as he said it. "Back garden might be a better option." He saw her confusion. "In the evening, cool air flows off the lake to the land. It's moist air, which feels even cooler. I'd suggest back yard."

Annie was silent too long.

"Something is on your mind. Don't worry. We'll make our own party."

"Not that."

"Your visitor."

"How did they know I'd been digging around in the missing persons and like that?"

"Probably had a bot looking for anyone searching the databases."

The Chilled Corpse

"A bot?"

"Think tracking cookies."

"That makes sense, I guess."

They chatted for another half hour about local events, past and present, on Labor Day.

"Gotta' go. I'll see you next Friday, then. What time?"

"I told John five-ish. Thanks for all." She ran out of words to express the many things she was thankful to Tom for.

"Nadda. Take care, keep your doors locked, at least for now."

After Tom left, she wandered the house, running her hands along the walls in the hallways. She went into the attic and walked the center of it, reacquainting herself with the items stored there, not opening any cupboards of chests, but recalling what she'd seen there, including the chest with the bones. After her stroll through the house, she went to the garden. There was a large flat spot near the end, wide open to the sky, where a campfire would not be a hazard. She went into the house and called Josie.

"Hey, there. I wonder. Do I need a permit to set up a campfire?"

"No, I doubt it. But go ahead and call the fire department. They'll tell you. I think you need a fire ring or a stone circle. Fire extinguisher, if you have one, buckets of water to put it out when done."

"You sound rushed. I'll let you go. Have a great day."

"Sorry. Yes. I've got six dozen cupcakes to make for an event. Talk to you later, yes?"

"Yes."

Annie sat in her library and watched her door cam view of dusk settling in. She then picked up the manual John had left because she wondered if she could record what the cams were seeing.

= = =

Chapter 17

The next morning, Annie was eager to get to work now that she had the hang of distribution.

She prepared a 'to go' cup of coffee and went out the door, focusing on getting it locked. When she turned to go to her car, she was startled by a flash of red down by the shore. Blood was her first thought, but she soon realized it was a coat on a man. She gasped. Her alarm hadn't alerted her to any unusual movement.

She stood on her step and focused on breathing while taking in the scene. The man was wearing the red jacket of a Canadian Mounted Police, with the leather belt and bandolier from one shoulder to the opposite waist, and the flat crown hat. Slowly, she went down the stairs.

The man turned his face slightly to show he knew she was coming, but made no other move. It was Andy.

Her steps were hesitant, but sure as she approached him.

He turned to her when she was still a few feet away. "Hello Annie. I didn't mean to scare you."

"Well and good you did. Why are you here?"

"I have a proposition for you."

"I'm listening. But if it has to do with not trying to figure out who the dead man is---was, then no deal."

"Good. I'd hoped you had a positive attitude."

Annie felt a smile chase across her face. "You are setting me up for something. I can feel it."

"I am. Come and sit. You have a few more minutes before Julie expects you."

"I do. You've been tracking me."

"It is what we do. Well, some of it."

"You are no longer undercover, I take it."

"I am not at the moment undercover. I am here in my official capacity. I had to get permission from your locals to be here, too. The Staties knew we were working in the area. They knew who George Gentry was. It is part of why you felt you were being stonewalled."

"Gene Gent?"

"Yes."

"He was undercover?"

"Yes, his whole group was."

"He wasn't killed at the Inn."

"No. His group needed somewhere to put him after he was killed. They needed to not blow their cover. We do know who he was and we know how he died."

"So why not tell me --- us. Dave apparently didn't know either." She sat on a rock facing him. "Why are you here, now?"

"Like I said, I have something to ask of you."

"Ask, then."

"One of Canada's natural resources is being siphoned off and shipped down to the states. We've tracked some of it to Bangor."

"Why are you in Abigale, then?"

"We needed a base away from the city, but within easy reach."

The Chilled Corpse

"Josie's Inn."

"Yes. It fit the bill. And it might be being funneled though here."

"So what do you need from me. Case solved?"

"No. We need someone from away, someone not known in the community, someone who can masquerade as well-to-do."

"And I fit the bill."

"And you are curious."

"I am. But how can I help." She recalled the cup she was still holding and took a sip to cover her nervousness.

"We want you to insert yourself into the situation. Make noise on your computer that you are looking to make some money from the property you just inherited. You are property rich and cash poor. Something like that."

"How will that help."

"When these people reach out to you, when they research you and find you have an isolated property with some potential for storage, they might bite."

"And I do what. I don't want any part of drug dealing. Those are dangerous people."

"Not drugs." When he smiled, it lit his face.

"Not drugs. What. You said a national treasure."

"Not a treasure, but a resource. Someone is illegally selling Canadian maple syrup. We haven't figured out how, just that it is coming through Bangor before moving down into the other states."

"Maple Syrup. Are you kidding!"

Andy shook his head. "No."

"How does a few gallons of a natural product threaten your national security?"

"It's not a few gallons, Annie. It is thousands and thousands of gallons."

"How would you even know? I thought a few people just did it for their own use?"

"It is big business. Like milk, producers sell their product to large firms. We first noticed a few years ago, that there seemed to be a scarcity, and chalked it up to a 'bad year'. But the scarcity seemed to be growing."

"How many people are shipping it out?"

"Not how many. I think the growers have no idea what's going on. And it is big business for some. The sugar bush farmers can own thousands of acres and get hundreds of thousands of gallons. They ship the raw product to distilleries who blend and concentrate the syrup and then bottle it for sale. Somewhere along that supply line, some of it is going missing."

"What does missing maple syrup have to do with me?"

"You can help us find out where it is coming from and where it is going and also help figure out who killed George." He stared off at the lake.

"He was someone you knew?"

"I did." He continued to look out at the lake.

The call of a single loon broke the silence.

Annie waited for the return call. It didn't come. The one loon called again from her right. There still was no answer and the loon flew from right to left, low and close to the water.

"That's the first time I've seen one fly."

"They can't fly in the summer. They lose their pin feathers."

Silence surrounded them again.

"All right. What exactly can I do to help?

"We'll make public that you have acquired a large property but need some cash, that you are looking for a way to generate money.

"Then what."

"Then we wait."

"And if someone wants to do business?"

"I'll go undercover as your special friend, I think. I'm not known around here. We will put trackers on it and watch where it goes."

Annie attempted to hide her blush by turning away from him. "Will I be in danger?"

"No. I don't think so. Someone will be here with you at all times."

"How do I explain that to friends?"

"You don't. We'll be almost invisible, except for me."

"Invisible. I'm having a party here on Monday."

"It will take at least that long to set this up. And we won't need to do anything until someone contacts you, in any case. But that would be a great time to introduce me to your friends."

"You say."

"I expect you won't hear much before mid-winter, when they are putting out feelers for next year. I've written up a small article to run, if you can get Julie to do it."

"No danger, you say?"

"No danger. Think about it. We have time." He stood, touched his cap, and gave a small bow. "I look forward to hearing from you. We'll make a fantastic fake couple, I think."

Her stomach gave a small twinge when he smiled at her.

"We'll see."

"Have a great day." He walked away, along the shore, following the path that Tom had shown her.

"That's why I didn't hear his car," she said to the empty air.

Andy spoke to her from among the bushes. "Oh, and thanks for being willing to help, Annie."

Her stomach flipped when he spoke her name. She could just make out the red coat through the brush.

"And I'll remind you that you don't mention this to anyone?"

Not sure if he could see her, she nodded.

"Monday, then." His red coat then disappeared as if by magic.

The lonely loon called once, and she watched as he flew back across the lake to the place he had come from. Had something happened to the mate, or had the mate flown? Maybe this was one or the youngsters, testing its wings for the long flight. Where did loons go in winter?"

Annie got in her car and went to work, her insides thrumming to the tune of the morning's encounter. A fake boyfriend. It was the theme of so many bad movies. A smile crept over her face from time to time as she sorted and delivered.

"I'll treat you at Josie's," said Julie when they were done.

The stopover at the Inn was becoming a pattern. Annie just wished she could share with her friend what had occurred that morning. The red coat down by the shoreline, the giddy feeling of doing something important and Andy as fake boyfriend were so fantastic as to feel unreal.

= = =

Chapter 18

The week quickly moved into Monday. Annie awoke eager to prep for the evening's festivities. Labor Day had never meant much to her, except for having a day off.

Andy arrived at noon. Dress slacks and a short-sleeved button down had replaced the red coat and he carried a bombardier style jacket.

Insides clenching, she greeted him. "How do we play this?"

"We 'play' this causal. I'm a friend of yours up for the week." Andy sat at the kitchen table as if he had been there for a long time.

"I'll follow your lead, then. I've never done anything like this." She turned to hide her alarm. 'Undercover' seemed a nasty word to her, bringing up images from adventure movies where someone always gets hurt. Although this felt special to her, he had probably done it more than a few times.

"We're friends. If anyone asks personal questions, you deflect. Suddenly, something needs your attention. We'll iron out the details in the upcoming week. It's better to just keep things vague and simple."

"I understand." Her heart beat too fast and her face flushed a little.

"Need help with anything? Chairs, table, anything?"

"I, ush! Folks will bring their own chairs. I set out the table earlier." Her eyes roamed the kitchen as she looked for something to keep busy. "I'll bring the food out later."

"What are we having?"

"We're having hot dogs, coleslaw, potato salad and S'mores."

The Chilled Corpse   Page 143

"I love S'mores. Hey, I know. Do you have the sticks for the marshmallows?"

Her hand went to her mouth in astonishment. "I hadn't thought."

"I'll go out and get some. You have excellent bushes along the path. How many folks are coming?"

"I think there'll be about eight. Oh, and you and me, too. So ten."

"I'll go do that and get them soaking. That will help keep them from burning." Smoothly, he stood and came to where she was standing near the stove. "Look. It'll be fine. You'll be fine." He patted her shoulder twice, then turned and went outside.

Taking a breath, Annie realized his presence had left her tense. What was she doing? The party was trying enough, but now to have to play out this charade would be really challenging.

For the tenth time, she checked a tray that held the condiments, napkins, plates, forks and spoons and cups. Did people at these events drink from cups or right from bottles. That brought up another question. Was Tom bringing bottles or cans. So much she didn't know. She should have asked. She sat at the kitchen table for a moment, picked up her phone to call Tom and ask about what he was bringing for drinks, but put the phone back down without dialing. He was going to bring what he would bring and she had no idea what was the correct thing, in any case.

Half an hour passed, with Annie double checking the food and the tray. Did she need to prep some ice? Should she have gotten some ice? Did they need a bucket or tub to put the drinks in. She'd seen movies where there was a large tub filled with ice and the drinks went in that. Would Tom put the drinks in the fridge? She had more questions than answers. Finally, she stood and went outdoors, almost crazy with anxiety.

Andy had a pile of sticks which he was sharpening. "Hey, there. I've gotten up a couple dozen. I'll soak them in the lake until S'mores time. Have you got some string or rope? I want to tie them together, so they don't float off."

"Yes." She pivoted and went back in and dug out a spool of fine string she'd inherited with the house.

"Will this do," she asked as she presented the ball of twine to him.

"Perfect. You'll be fine. This will go well. You've got this."

"I do?" She took a deep breath. "I do. I've got this. These are my friends."

"Let's go by the water. I find the water soothes."

"It does. I want to get a boat next year. Something small. There's a small motor for boats in the shed behind the house."

"Can I see?"

"Sure." Leading the way, Annie showed him her shed, one of several on the property.

"This is old. Maybe from the sixties. Wow. Nice." He gave a test pull. "With your permission, I can get this up and running for you. It pulls good. Nothing is bound up in it."

"That might be nice." Suddenly aware that they were in a small, confined space alone, she stepped out of the shed.

Andy followed and closed the shed up. "This shed is very close to the house, closer than I'd like, but there's the boat shed and there's also that mini barn over near the woods. But we can also offer the use of the small greenhouse up at the end of the garden. I have no idea how much storage they'll want, since we have no clue if the product comes in and goes right back out or is stored in situ until called for. Currently the thought is that it is only temporarily housed in the area before being shipped on to whatever market they are using."

"Sounds complicated." She walked back around the house and sauntered down to the water's edge.

Silently, companionably, the two sat. Annie glanced at her phone, checking the time and for messages, fearing cancelations would come in and her 'party' would be a bust.

"Don't do that."

"Do what?"

"Keep checking the time. In my work, I have found that it leads to a higher stress level. Just be. Be in the moment. Enjoy the things around you. This is a lovely place, by the way. I'll greatly enjoy being here."

"I'm glad."

The ducks came paddling by.

"Almost full grown. They'll go about mid-October in this region. The water gets colder, and the fish go deeper so food gets scarce. The loons will go before that. Canadian Geese usually leave about that time, too."

"I wondered."

The ducks had wended along the shoreline and were out of site when they heard the first car come down the lane.

"Tom, of course. He said he'd help. Here we go, then. You are my friend, up for the week?"

"That will work."

She took a deep breath and looked down at her feet to steady herself.

"Go. I'll stay here for a few moments. You'll be fine."

"I know. These are friends." She wanted to say more but there were no words. She turned to the driveway. "Hey, there Tom."

He was pulling something from his trunk by the time she reached his car. "Oh, nice."

"Got two different beers and assorted soft drinks." He pulled a plastic tub from the trunk. "Here, if you'll carry this tub, we'll set up."

It only took a few minutes to transport the supplies to the garden area. Soon, the tub had water and ice and drinks.

"You already have a guest?"

Just then, Andy rounded the corner of the house.

Annie introduced Tom to Andy. "My friend who heard about my party and decided to join me for a few days."

Andy stuck out his hand. "Hey, glad to meet you. I've heard lots about this special guy named Tom."

"Oh? What, exactly," he asked with a chuckle.

"I'll never tell," quipped Andy, also with a chuckle.

By five o'clock, the yard was abuzz with visitors.

Pulling her aside, Josie asked softly. "Tell. This is a big secret. Is he someone special?"

Remembering the agreement to keep things simple and plain, Annie shrugged. "Just a friend. Up for a week or so."

The Chilled Corpse

"Sure," replied Josie. "Not special, she says."

"Just a friend," answered Annie, but feeling a blush spread over her face.

Joanne followed Annie into the house to help carry out the food while the rest of the company set up chairs around the table.

Andy took lead on bringing wood out of the shed and setting things up. "Hey, Tom. Want to help set up the campfire?" Soon, a blaze was going.

Annie felt a jostle of competition between Andy and Tom, almost a contest for the dominant male position. She didn't know how to handle it.

John came up and whispered softly in her hear. "They'll settle in. Tom has been the caretaker around here and he feels a little displaced, and apparently Andy wants to establish that he's the man of the house."

Smiling, Annie responded. "Well, neither one is, actually, I think. But point well taken."

The evening went off better than Annie had hoped. After the first round of checking each other out, the men settled down and seemed to be enjoying great camaraderie, easy in each other's presence. Annie had seen .John speak softly to Tom but hadn't heard what he'd said, so she suspected he'd had a hand in the two men getting along better.

As the evening progressed, the air got cooler. S'mores were a hit as people pulled up closer to the fire for warmth.

Faces blurred in the firelight and laughter burbled up from the group enjoying each other's company. Andy seemed to fit right in, helping with the marshmallows and crackers and chocolate, fetching drinks, and as people were leaving, helping to bring things indoors.

"A success?"

"Yes," answered Annie. "A definite success."

When the last item had been brought in and taken care of, panic struck with enough force to clench her stomach and catch her breath. 'Where was Andy going to sleep?' She hadn't prepared a place for him.

Almost as if reading her mind, he spoke up. "If it's all right with you, I want to sleep in the library, near your computer. I'll get my bedroll from the car."

Annie looked away so he wouldn't see the relief.

"Tomorrow, we'll get my computer set up to your security system and I'll be able to take one of the bedrooms upstairs, if that's all right."

"Yes," she finally choked out. "I just hadn't thought ahead. My mother would have had that all sorted."

"Really. I'll be fine in the library. The article won't run until Thursday, or even next week, anyway, but we don't' know who the players are and I just want to be sure."

"That's fine, then. And thank you for the help this evening. It did go well, didn't it."

"I like your friends. Now, if I may, I'll get my stuff, and I'd like a shower, if that's not a problem."

Annie nodded.

"Good night, then."

"Good night, Andy. And thanks again."

"I enjoyed it. Thank you."

= = =

Chapter 19

Tuesday morning, Annie lay abed wallowing in joy at the success her first event at her house had been. She pulled up the sheets and gazed out the window at the tops of the trees down by the lake. A warm feeling enveloped her as she thought about the friends she'd acquired in the short time she'd lived here.

Abigale was such a kind cozy town. She delighted in the idea that she would live here the rest of her life. She sat bolt upright as the memory of Andy mingling with those friends slammed into her, taking her breath away. Then she recalled it was Tuesday, distribution day, and Julie would expect her.

She sat in the bed for a full minute as she wondered where 'he' was in the house at this very moment. The sound of water in the pipes in the downstairs bathroom told her. She quickly got dressed, brushing her hands through her hair as she went downstairs.

The scent of brewing coffee wafted to her when she arrived at the landing. She inhaled deeply to clear her thoughts as well as savor the rich sweetness of someone else fixing her morning brew.

Andy almost collided with her when she reached the door to the bathroom. "Sorry. I didn't know you were up." His hair was still wet from his shower, but he was fully dressed in clothes much like what he'd had on last night.

"I see you've made yourself at home." The sentence sounded much harsher than she'd intended.

"Sorry if that wasn't proper."

"No, it's fine. Sorry." She skated around him and into the kitchen.

He followed. "I hope you don't mind that I started some coffee. Neat machine."

"Yes. I like it. Just got my stuff up from New York. Tom came and helped. He was a great help." Realizing she was nervously rambling, she snapped her lips shut.

"May I make you some breakfast?"

"Go ahead if you want some. I usually don't' eat much until later, and then just a sandwich or something."

"I'll fix us some brunch later, if that's all right."

"It will be nice to have someone else cook for a change, but I have to go to work." She felt a further need to explain. "In the city, usually I would have grabbed something on the way to work. I didn't cook much. I'm sort of just learning to bake. Josie is teaching me some."

"I like to cook. It's calming. I can't always get access to a kitchen when I'm on the job." He poured them some coffee and put the mugs on the table.

Sitting across from him, looking at his deep blue eyes, she wondered about his home life. Wife kids or did he live with his parents? Sitting across from her guest made the situation all too real. "What now?" She looked over at the burbling coffee machine to avoid the near perfect chin and lips.

"Now, we wait. Did Julie give you any indication if the story we prepared for you will run?"

Her gaze was pulled back to him. "Oh, yes. I'm supposed to bring her a picture of the house to run with it. She's made a few modifications, thinking I'd written it. She put in that friends had helped me move in. She commented that I was delighted to be living here and that's why I had thrown a picnic party and she also mentioned that it was a success. It ends with just a sentence that I'm currently employed by the paper."

"As long as she left in the part that the house has lots of potential and you are exploring ways to gain some income from it."

"Yes. Will that be enough?"

"I suspect it will."

They sat quietly for a few minutes.

Annie wondered how long it would take and if Andy would be there all that time, and if it would be this awkward all that time.

"If you don't mind, I 'd like to go tinker on that outboard."

"Outboard?"

"The boat motor in your near shed."

"Oh, sure. Go for it. I'll have my money for a boat next summer."

"Have you spoken to many about the inheritance?"

"No. Tom knows, of course, and Joe Johnson, the attorney, and I'm not sure, but Josie might know."

"The fewer the better. It will make this more attractive. We'll run another article next month, if we haven't had any results, yet."

The timeline startled her, and she accidentally slammed her cup onto the table.

Andy misinterpreted her nerves. "Don't' worry. Someone will be here all the time with you. When I can't be here, someone else will sub in."

The Chilled Corpse

The statement did not calm her nerves. She blurted out "It's just that I'm used to living alone."

"Oh."

"I can do it. For a short time. It's a big house. And I need to get used to it if I plan on running a B&B or something." Her hands twisted around her cup. As she gazed down at the empty mug, she registered that he had stood.

He carefully placed his used coffee cup in the sink.

Clearing her throat, Annie started to speak but her voice broke. She started again. "I'm sorry. I didn't mean to offend. I'm not very good at dealing with people. It has always been numbers for me."

Andy came back to the table and sat on the edge of his chair. He took her hand in his. "Look, I know I'm a stranger, and that this is an odd situation. We won't let anything happen to you, and we'd do it another way, if we could. But once this is set in motion, we'd like to see it through. If you want to bail, now would be the time."

She looked up and saw the empathy in his eyes. "I'm fine. I want to do this. It will work out." A smile tweaked the corners of her mouth. "After all, I'd always wanted to be an investigator in finances, you know, nail the bad guys because of faulty bookkeeping, or shady dealings, stuff like that."

"Like Al Capone, or like Martha Stewart?"

"Yes." The smile spread across her face. "Just as long as someone is around."

"There will be. I'm pretty sure they'll bite, and then we can end the drain on Canada's natural resource."

"Natural resource." A thought occurred to her. "Do I have any maples?"

"I'm sure you do."

"Could I be getting some syrup from them?"

"You could."

"Is that something I should be concerned with right away? I guess I could wait until next year."

"It's done in the spring, when the sap just starts to run. When nights are still freezing, but the days are warm. The syrup is no longer good after the nights warm up."

"Oh. Should that all be set up before the freeze? I see pictures of miles of blue tubing."

"You can tap just a single tree. With a bucket. I'll help you research it. But it gets set up in the spring."

"But there's snow on the ground, then."

"Yes. It makes it difficult. Those who have many trees do lay out the lines in the fall, but most don't tap the trees, that is insert the spigots, until spring."

"Wow. I never thought about the work involved."

"I'll go try to get the outboard running. Then we can google maple syrup production. It is a lot of work. It's not for everyone."

"Later, then."

Andy strolled out.

Annie went to work. The morning seemed so normal she almost forgot about the drama at her house. At Josie's Inn, over a doughnut and coffee, she blushed as the thought of

Andy in her home and the secrets she was keeping flitted through her thoughts.

Back at the house, she rattled around the house. She knew Andy was around because his car was in the driveway. How might she please him and make him feel more at home? "Muffins. I'll bet he likes muffins."

An old cookbook she found had recipes for dozens of different muffins. At first glance they seemed so different, but she remembered Josie's guidance. The basics were the same. Although the book listed ingredients in different order, she came to see the pattern. Flour, a liquid, a flavoring agent like cinnamon or cloves or lemon and maybe an ingredient, like apple, or pear or blueberries. She had apples. Soon, the whole house was redolent of baked goods. The toothpick test showed they were done.

Andy entered just as she was taking them out of the oven. "You have a great little machine there. The shear pin was broken. Someone hit a rock or something. An easy fix. I'll pick some up next time I'm in town."

Annie almost dropped the muffin tin. "Town?"

"We do have to go from time to time."

"Oh. Yes." The vision of being left alone at the house faded when she realized he had included her. "I'll have to go tomorrow. Julie wants some 'back to school' pictures and a picture of the house to go with the article."

"I'll help with that. We'll get an angle that shows at least one of the sheds. Those smell delicious."

"I hope you like apple cinnamon. I added a bit more cinnamon, because one teaspoon didn't seem like enough, but then I think it's too much."

"I love cinnamon."

The muffins were great.

"I think Julie will run the article in Thursday's paper. Then we wait?"

"Then we wait. I've been tidying up your sheds for you. Things have been left in a jumble. And your lawn needs a good mowing, too."

"Yes. And yes." She laughed. "I'll tidy up here and join you soon."

He nodded and went out the door.

Annie took a deep breath. This wasn't going to be so bad, after all. Andy was easy. She hoped the replacements would be as nice.

Outside, after cleaning up the kitchen, she heard Andy tossing things around in the shed right behind the house. She joined him. "Do you want to do anything with this old dryer? I can take it to the dump for you. I plugged it in and it doesn't work. I noticed you have one in the house."

"Oh, please."

"I hung this old chain up. There are several long pieces. I put them on different hooks, so they don't get tangled again."

Item after item, they sorted, hung or put in the discard pile. A space opened up in the center, and then spread outwards until most of the shed was clear of items.

"Time for a break, and maybe more muffins. To go with supper. Those are good."

"Yes. Let's"

= = =

Chapter 20

The next morning, Annie got her pictures of the Dower House for Julie, but not without some input from Andy.

"Here, let me," he finally said.

Annie viewed his shots of how he thought the property should be displayed and she had to admit he was good with a camera. "I'll delete most of mine, so Julie will choose one of yours."

"Sorry. I didn't mean to take over."

"Your fine." She looked up and saw he was watching her reactions. "You are fine. It's all good. You're good with a camera. I can see from your shots what it is you wanted to display. I was more focused on the house itself, and you wanted to show off the whole property."

"Yes. So, we go to town now?"

"Yes. We go to town now."

His smile lit up his face.

Annie felt a small tremor in her belly at that smile which made him not only more handsome but youthful. Again, she wondered about his conjugal status.

Julie was pleased with the pictures, but had no time to visit, with a deadline in just a few hours. The printing company would need all the articles and layout by five PM. The crew at that facility would work through the night, editing out any errors, and then actually printing the paper and stacking. Delivery usually arrived at y seven the Abigale Gazette office by seven in the morning.

"Now, we wait," said Andy, when she got back in the car.

"We wait." She twiddled her car keys a moment before putting them in the ignition. "Shall we drop in on Josie?"

"I have a few errands to run. Get that shear pin, for starters. You go ahead and visit with your friend."

Annie didn't want to show relief that he wasn't going to shadow her every minute, but she was a bit anxious that he wouldn't. She reassured herself that it was too early to worry, in any case and responded positively. "Say hi to John and Joanne, then?"

"Sure. See you out front of the Inn."

"Will do."

Josie was busy prepping to cater a business meeting the next morning but took a few minutes to sit with Annie and a cup of tea and some fruit bars that were fresh out of the oven.

"Nice party, girl."

"I enjoyed it." A smile wreathed her face at the memory.

"Everyone else seemed to. Now tell about that handsome 'friend' you've kept under wraps."

Annie wanted to blurt out the truth and instead she bit her lower lip gently and shrugged. "Andy is just a friend. From away. He heard about the party and decided to come." She clamped her teeth to avoid saying more, remembering Andy's advice to keep it simple.

"Well, let me know if it isn't going to go anywhere, because I might take a spin around with him."

"Oh, you."

"So, how long will he be around?"

"I'm not sure." Be vague, Andy had said.

The Chilled Corpse   Page 159

"Gotta' get busy, now. But bring him by on Friday for our buffet."

"Maybe." Annie smiled up at her friend. "We might just do that."

Back at the house, Andy went to the shed to finish fixing the outboard motor and Annie went in the house. She found herself pacing, wishing the paper was already out and that she already was done with all the high drama it might bring. She paced and then started dusting and ran the vacuum on the stairs and hallway, then through the empty rooms on either side of the hall. In the library, she saw Andy's bedroll and remembered she wanted to fix up a bedroom for him. After she had and finished that project, time was still heavy.

"Supper. For two. How strange." Soon, she had a robust chicken stew in the crockpot and dove down the rabbit hole of recipe books, thinking she wanted to make biscuits but wasn't sure of the recipe. Scones, biscuits, and muffins all seem to be about the same. Finally, she quit, just as Andy entered.

"Smells great. I'll just go for a wash up, if that's all right." He sniffed his hands. "I smell of gasoline."

"Get it running?"

"It's a great machine. You should get many more years out of it."

"Next year, a boat to put it on." She fiddled with a cookbook cover. "Oh, and I put you in one of the upstairs bedrooms. We'll hook up your computer this evening?"

"Great. I'll only be a few."

When Andy returned, hair still damp, a different colored shirt but the same color of pants, Annie almost snorted with repressed giggles. Did he have a trunk full of the same clothing in different colors?

"I'm funny?"

"No. Just, you always look the same, except when in your uniform, that is." The giggles dissipated as she recalled who he was and why he was here. "Chicken stew for supper."

"Great. Look, we can take turns cooking, if you want. I don't want to be a burden, or I can fix my own meals. I can go into the city tomorrow and stock up."

"We can go later in the week. I need some things, too. We can do a list up together." She gathered the cookbooks.

Andy sat at the table.

Annie restacked the cookbooks, then looked up at Andy. "We'll make a list."

"You already said that. Do I make you nervous? Is my being here too much? I can move into one of the sheds, keep a low profile."

"No. It's good. You're good. No, heck no. I'm just not used to having someone around." She almost added 'someone handsome'.

"We'll make up a list and sort who will make meals when." He took her hand off the cookbooks she had restacked a second time. "This will work out. We'll be good."

The Bangor Daily News picked up the story of the orphaned descendant of a state resident *come home* and used the same picture that had been published in the Gazette.

The week passed quickly. When Annie went to the office, Andy followed into town and spent time at Josie's or shopping, meeting the townsfolks.

The Chilled Corpse   Page 161

Back at the house, he kept busy with minor repairs that Tom hadn't done, yard work or spent time out by the lake. In his second week there, he came home from town with fishing equipment. His third week, he had Annie choose paint for of the sheds and scraped and painted those.

Josie questioned her several times about Andy and Annie kept her answers vague. Tom sometimes came out to check on her, but not as often as before Andy had arrived.

Annie felt her nerves fraying from having him underfoot all the time.

Andy spent more time down by the shore as the weeks went on.

At breakfast one morning, Andy broached the topic that was on both their minds. "I think we may have to consider that no one will reach out."

"Andy, why did you choose Abigale and why me?"

"We suspected that the goods were being run through here in the past. And you seemed a great choice, great back story."

"And dumb as nails, pliable, eager to go along with this cockamamie scheme of yours. Don't you have someone back home missing you?"

"No. Oh, no. My mom is used to me being away and I don't have any pets." The sparkle in his eyes told her he knew what she was asking and wasn't giving it to her.

"No one special?"

"No one special." He lost his smile. "Look. Let's give it another week. That will push it into October."

"Yes. I'm aware."

"If we don't hear by then, I'll leave."

Her whole body tensed at the thought that they had maybe set something in motion, and he wouldn't be around when someone came calling.

"All you'd have to do is give a call if anyone reaches out, and I can be here in literally no time."

"Like how long, no time."

"A couple hours."

Over a second cup of coffee, they discussed the logistics of it, how she could get in touch with him, how to delay encounters with anyone making contact and back up plans.

"I'm reluctant to loop in the locals. We just don't know who might be involved. The State Troopers know I'm working in the area, but don't know where or on what."

"You suspect that someone from this town is involved, someone I've met since coming here, maybe even one of my friends."

His face told her all she didn't want to know about his thinking.

"You do think that, don't you."

He wiped his hand across his face as they sat over his empty cup. "I don't know anything. That's the problem."

Annie stood and slammed her cup into the sink. "I've had enough, then. No more. Just, I think you need to leave. I think this isn't going to work out. I don't think anyone is going to contact me to use this property to hide your precious maple syrup. I want to be done with this all."

Andy stood and walked up behind her, leaving a foot between them. "I know this has been stressful. You agreed to the plan and I'd told you it might be a long game." He nodded once. "I understand. I thank you for allowing the chance, anyways. "I'll go tomorrow."

Without turning around, she nodded. "Fine."

He started to walk off. "

She turned to him. "And Andy, it hasn't been a bother to have you here. I've enjoyed the company. I just don't want any part of this anymore. I thought we'd do it, someone would reach out, we'd nab them and it would be over." She smiled at him gently. "I'm sorry it didn't work out the way you wanted.

"Me, too. I'm going fishing." He smiled ruefully and turned sharply and left the kitchen. A few minutes later, she heard the door open and close.

"Whoosh. After all, enough is enough," she said to the empty kitchen. Relief at the thought that he was leaving and this entire fiasco would be done was over ridden by the sense of loss at his leaving. Confusion swirled her into a cleaning frenzy and she scrubbed the kitchen top to bottom in her attempt to clear the thoughts churning in her brain.

= = =

Chapter 21

Annie had finished scrubbing down the kitchen and was contemplating a good dusting of the library when the security system alerted her to a car in the driveway. Thinking Andy might be going somewhere, she brought up the image of her yard. It was Tom, coming in. She expected to see Andy down by the shore, but he wasn't visible, and she wondered where he was. He sometimes went along the shore path either fishing or going for a walk.

She met Tom at the door. "Hello, there stranger."

"Hey, there." He seemed hesitant, a half-smile on his face.

"Come in. I was just about to have a cup of tea."

"Gladly. I see your guest is still here."

"He's out fishing at the moment."

Tom followed her into the kitchen. "Smells like cleaner."

Glad to see Tom, but at a loss for words, she stated the obvious. "I just cleaned the kitchen." She put water on to boil. "Regular black, green, herb, blueberry or sleepy time?"

"Not sleepy time. Please. I'd like the fruit one, I think." He sat and watched her for a moment. "Annie, are you all right? You've seemed tense since your friend arrived."

"I'm fine." She stopped and looked at him, leaning on the counter while waiting for the water to heat. She turned back and took down two mugs and set the tea things on the table. Without looking at Tom, she spoke again. "Andy will be leaving tomorrow." Then she turned slowly to see the reaction.

"I see. And just a friend, you said?"

"Yes. We're not, like involved, if that's what you want to know." She watched him to see what effect the news might have.

"I came out today on an errand. Well, it's two errands."

Annie heart rate stepped up. It was always a possibility that someone she knew was involved in the illegal funneling of goods from Canada and the death of Gene, aka George. Could it be Tom?

Tom fiddled with his spoon. Then he looked up at her, gripping her attention. "I've had two different people approach me in the past because I was caretaker. Now, I want to present it to you, but I'm confused. The paper article said you were thinking about ways to have this place make money. I've told you, that once you've been here for six months, you won't ever need income again. You'll have the endowment."

"Yes, you've told me." Her heart beat double time. Was he somehow involved? Was Tom about to reveal the truth?

"I have but it sounds like you want to somehow have this place make some money. The newspaper article brought two people to my door, asking about it, since they know me, not you, and know I was caretaker over here and I'm familiar with the property."

"Two?" She set the filled cups on the table with the tea bags in them and sat opposite him, gripping her cup to stop her hands from shaking.

"John and his wife run the hardware but are looking to branch out. They can't do it at the current location, due to the lease and contract with Ace Hardware, who own the building."

Annie busied herself with her teacup, adding honey, trying not to let him see her nervousness.

"They want to run a secondhand shop." He fiddled with his cup, then looked up. "Old fashioned hand tools and things."

"And how does this concern me?"

"They thought, maybe one of your outbuildings would suit. I think the boat shed would be about the right size and easily accessed from the driveway." He took a sip and put the cup back down deliberately. "I can pitch it to them, if you like. Their store is about dried up and they see this as a sort of retirement income." He watched for her reaction.

Annie nodded once. "I like them. Are you sure that's what they want?"

"They've been talking about it for a few years now. What do you mean, is that what they want?"

"I just want to be sure of their intentions. I wouldn't want ---." She paused. She'd almost blurted out 'for my property to be used for illegal purposes', because of course, that was exactly what the article and Andy presence were about.

"Wouldn't want what."

"I wouldn't want strangers taking up residence, I guess."

"They'd pay something, of course, but wouldn't be able to afford much. That's why the thought of renting from you is so appealing. They'd be open mostly on weekends, yard sale style, and also selling on the internet." He twiddled his cup, then looked up. "If it gets too much, we can set them up with some other arrangement somewhere else. I personally think you'd do well to have more people around." He waited to see how she answered.

"I'll give it some thought. It should be fine. And it would be a great use for the boat house, which already has tool boards with those hangers and shelves and a workbench."

"And it's a great setting. But only if you are sure."

"It might work. I'll give it some thought."

"Do you have to run that *'thought'* by your *'friend'*?"

"Andy? No. It's not like that. Told you he's leaving tomorrow." She finished her tea in one long gulp. "It'll be fine to have someone around more. You've been busy? I haven't seen much of you."

"I've wanted to give you and your friend space."

"Don't be like that, Tom." She stood and carried the two empty cups to the sink. "I told you," she said, her back still to him. "Andy is just a friend."

"And he's leaving tomorrow."

"Yes." She turned around. "You said two errands?"

"Yes. My Accountant, Marc, and his wife run an antique store. They have a building, sometimes run auctions, are open weekends, stuff like that. But they need some storage. A place to put stuff that they aren't currently listing, stuff that maybe needs fixing, or the like." He twisted in his seat to look at her more squarely. "They just want storage space. They'd thought of renting a self-storage unit in the city, but this would be more convenient."

"Marc and his wife?" Her heart started to trip hammer again. "Rent storage?"

"You met them. They were here to help you move in."

"Oh, yes. I remember. She's runner lean and he's a bit portlier. They often stood very near each other when in the same room."

"That's them. A habit of a lifetime."

"Again, I'll think about it, but I could probably let them have the barn, out near the woods. The greenhouse wouldn't do, as I think the mice like that building."

"They do that. I've tried to eradicate them. They just come back and I gave up. As long as they stay there."

Annie sat back at the table. "Honestly. I don't need all this space. My apartment in the city. Well, you saw it."

"I did."

"I think it might be nice to share out some of the space. For a fee, of course." She smiled at him and saw him relax.

"For a fee, of course. I can tell them and set it up. Draw up papers and make it official."

"I think that might be nice."

"When."

Confused, she stared at him. "When what?" The vision of folks bringing in five-gallon pails of maple syrup drifted through her thoughts.

Tom now looked confused. "When can they start using the outbuildings?"

"When? Oh, when. Anytime, I guess. Just anytime."

"Anytime what?" Andy had entered and now stood in the kitchen door.

Tom looked at Andy for several heartbeats, then answered him. "Oh, we're finalizing plans to have some of the

The Chilled Corpse

buildings rent out to some locals. Nothing that would concern you, I guess." Tom then attempted to soften his comment. "Catch any fish?"

"No. I wasn't trying very hard. And it's getting late in the season. They've gone deeper in the colder water."

He turned back to Annie. "So, I can tell them both yes?"

"Yes. You can tell them that." She shot a quick look at Andy, then returned her eyes to Tom. "I'll be happy to have people around, I think."

"I'll get back with you when I've got the paperwork." He stood. "See you in a few days, then."

"I'll be at Josie's, I think, for Friday supper."

Tom nodded and left the room.

Annie heard the front door open and close.

"What was that about?"

"I'll be renting out two of the buildings on the property. The boat house will be used as a secondhand store by John and Joanne of the hardware, tools and the like. And then Marc, the accountant, and his wife run an antique store and need more storage."

"Could either one be our culprit?"

"I doubt it. Both couples run legitimate business."

"Accounting doesn't' pay what it used to and aren't John and Joanne planning on retirement?"

"Were you listening at the peephole?" She tried to lighten the words with a smile.

"No. John spoke to me about it when I was in this week."

"I see. Tom is going to draw up the leases for me."

"I heard."

"Neither of them is your smuggler."

"Could be. That is, could be they are not."

"I think this is a dead end to your investigation. If you haven't found your murderer and smugglers, it could be they've moved on."

"Could be that. In any case, I'll check in with you from time to time, if that's all right, just to be sure."

"Just to be sure." Sadness at Andy's departure warped the smile she attempted to flash at him. She had enjoyed having him in the house, working on the property as he lingered, but also felt inhibited. He was so handsome, and polite and kind. She would miss him, and yet felt a quiver of relief that he'd be gone. Maybe it was because his leaving signaled the end of the smuggler magnet they had attempted to set up or because her attraction to him was a botherance she didn't need.

He stood. "I'll go pack my things. I want to leave early tomorrow. This evening, we'll be sure all your security is up to par and aligned."

"Sure." Annie followed him out of the kitchen and went into the library when he went upstairs.

= = =

Chapter 22

Andy left early Wednesday morning on a cold late September day.

By the time Annie arose, he was gone, his room empty and tidy, only the fishing pole left behind and a short note on the dresser.

'Thanks for the visit. I enjoyed my time here. You have been a great hostess. I'm leaving the fishing pole. I have others. See you some other time, if I get over this way again.' It was signed with a flourish, Andy.

The note could have been from a guest at a bed and breakfast like Josie's. She realized she'd hoped for a deeper connection, but remined herself that for him, this had been an assignment, an attempt to find out who had killed his friend and co-worker.

The day seemed drab and empty without Andy there . In addition, his vigor had accomplished many projects around the property.

After brunch, she took a cup of coffee and went out to her rock to watch the lake. The waves were white capped and angry. Finally, chilled, she went back inside, and wandered the halls aimlessly, before going into the library.

Outbuildings. Rent outbuildings. Two of them. She liked John and Joanne and having them around would be nice. From what Tom had said, Marc and Annette would not be around very much, just storing stuff, sometimes being in and out, but it would still be humans on the property.

As she envisioned what that would be like, she marveled that the previous owners, Anita and then Kelly Marie, had never used the property to make money. They must have had enough of it available. That brought her thoughts around to how Lucien was making a living, what exactly did he do in Boston.

Tom was waiting for her at Josie's on Friday when she arrived. He had papers in hand and before supper was served, the contracts for the two buildings were signed.

"I'll get their signatures tonight or tomorrow. I believe that J & J will be here tonight."

"Good." Now that the project was a reality, Annie couldn't seem to generate any enthusiasm for it.

The next day, John showed up at the house. "Joanne is really excited to be setting up shop here. We're going to close the store just after Christmas. Before the New Year. We could have done so any time in the last few years. Corporate was after us to close, but we just weren't ready. Would you mind if we painted?" They were outside the boathouse that would now be used for a second-hand shop. "I see the outside has been painted and it matches up with the house. We wouldn't want to change that."

"Yes. No, don't want to change that. Andy painted it while he was here." She realized she was missing him. "Well, if you have no customers, you can fish."

"Fish?" He gazed out at the lake. "Oh, fish. Yes. Might build a boat, if that's all right."

"I've wanted to have a boat."

"I can build a dock, too, this winter, if you want. There used to be one here tons of years ago."

"I can picture that. Yes. Sure." She felt she ought to be more enthused about John's winter projects that would enhance life at the Dower.

Joanne showed up the next week with a couple of buckets of paint and the things she'd need for the project.

Annie visited for a few minutes before going off to the office.

Joanne was gone when she came back home. Most of the inside had been transformed into sunshine yellow and deep blues of the lake. She'd drawn some ducks with green rings around the neck and some lifelike loons on one wall. Annie went into the house before phoning the store. "Great, wonderful. This is gorgeous. You didn't tell me you were an artist."

"I just copied some pictures from a book."

What did they call an abrupt change of place or circumstance? Future shock? Annie decided that was what ailed her. The house was clean, fresh paint on the woodwork, thanks to Andy, and little things had been tweaked to work better.

As the month morphed into October, she started questioning her perception of Andy, his plan to coax out some smugglers and wondered if he even was truly a Mountie, despite having seen him in uniform, or if he had really been on assignment at the time he was in Maine. Were they allowed to operate stateside? Maybe he had been part of the smuggling ring. How could she find out?

On October 3, a Tuesday, after the distribution and a photo assignment at the high school of the school library student staff, she returned to Josie's, troubled by her thoughts.

"Back so soon," teased Josie. "You'll have to watch me put together a few batches of Whoopie Pies, I'm afraid." She sat at a table. "Want anything?"

"I want to talk with you."

"About the mysterious Andy?"

"No. Yes. Did you ever hear any more about the guy we found in your cooler?"

"No. And I don't want to or need to. Thank You very much." She went to stand, then sat back down. "Look, I didn't know him, and I don't want to know anything about him. He obviously knew some dangerous people. Leave it. Just leave it."

"I need to tell you something. About Andy. I don't know if I'm just naïve, of if I was being led about."

"Strung along? How long have you known him, and where did you meet him?" She fiddled with the salt and pepper shakers on the table. Then she looked up at Annie. "I told you that if you weren't interested, I'd like to take a stab."

"He's gone now. He was only here for business."

"And what business was that. Not much going on in Abigale."

"You can't tell anyone." She stared at Josie."

Josie nodded that she understood and made a zipping her lips motion.

"He claims he's a Mountie."

"Mountie?"

"Yes. Royal Canadian Mounted Police."

"Holy Crow!" He hands went to her mouth, then down to the table. "Do tell."

"He came to me after, you know. The first time, he was dressed plain, like you've seen him. But then he appeared at the lake in his uniform. He claims to be investigating some smuggling."

"Are they allowed to work this side of the border?"

The Chilled Corpse

"He told me that the Staties were aware of his work here."

"Sounds like you aren't sure."

"I'm not sure. He could even be part of the ring doing the smuggling, which I think is tied to the death of that man. He told me he was friends with him and his name is, was George Gentry."

"Did he mention who he thinks killed 'his friend'."

"No. He didn't even mention it except that one time."

"Oh. Oh, I get it. That's why it said in the paper that you were looking for ways to make money from your 'recently acquired' property."

"I'm not sure of anything, right now. "

"Annie, you have to talk with Tom." She punctuated the comment with a nod. "Soon."

= = =

Chapter 23

"Tom, Josie suggested I come to talk with you. But first, I have to tell you a tall tale. But you can't tell anyone. I'm not supposed to talk about it." They were seated in his living room, crowded with two easy chairs, a huge old-fashioned oak desk, some books shelves and several tables stacked with more books. A coffee table held two cups and a carafe of coffee. "You remember Andy?"

"Yes. I understand he's gone. You told me you and he weren't involved. Are you changing your story?"

"No. We weren't, but I didn't tell you everything."

"Go on."

"He's a Mountie."

"Naw. Oh, shoot. I knew there was something buttoned down about him. But how'd you get to meet him?" He leaned forward in his chair, eager for her answer.

"He introduced himself to me. He simply arrived at the house and asked me to do something for him."

"What. That's incredible. What exactly--- Does it have to do with the dead person at Josie's? Why not approach her?"

"Yes, and no. I'm not supposed to---He asked me not to tell anyone. It seems there's been some smuggling going on. Some stuff coming in from Canada. Andy thought it came though Abigale. Josie said I needed to talk with you."

He didn't answer but picked up his cup slowly from the table and then leaned back in his chair "I'm listening.".

Annie told of the scheme to offer up her property for use and how that hadn't worked out, since no one had approached her. "Why did Josie suggest I talk with you, though?"

The Chilled Corpse

Tom came to his feet slowly and placed his cup on the tray deliberately, eyes down on his cup. His gaze stayed on the cup as he sat back down. When his eyes met hers, she saw alarm

He sipped his coffee, eyes on his cup. Then he looked up at her with big puppy eyes. "You have to understand. The property was empty for a long time. We couldn't find any heirs for years. I had charge of it, as well as finding you."

The hairs on her arms raised up. "Tom?"

"I allowed certain people to 'use' the property and didn't ask many questions. For instance, John kept a fishing boat out there. We removed it when we knew you were coming up."

"He did ask if he could build one and keep it there next summer. Did he use the boathouse for yard sales, already, before?"

"No. He didn't. But others did use the property, for something else. I'd rent out the barn from time to time. I never saw anyone around but could see it was used." He looked Annie in the eye for a full minute, waiting to see her reaction before breaking eye contact, then glanced back at her. "Wait. Has this anything to do with your dead man?"

"Not 'my' dead man. And I think so. What was being stored in the barn?"

"I don't know. I didn't ask. It was in barrels. Blue drums, maybe 20 or 30 gallon size." His eyes wandered the walls around them. He spoke to Annie without looking at her. "I should have, I suppose. I just---I just thought, I guess, that it was some outfit from Bangor, looking for a bit of industrial storage. "

He put his cup back and the table and stayed leaning forward as he explained. "The barrels usually came in the spring and were typically gone before first snow. I didn't think it was drugs, you see. Not in that kind of storage. I thought maybe cooking oil for a restaurant, or something." He looked at her again. "Honest. I didn't think it through. There was this space, no one using it and I didn't see any harm in having it used. Nothing, I mean nothing, set off alarms that it might be something illegal. I should have asked more questions."

"I hear you, though I don't fully understand. But I hear you."

"Do you know what was in the barrels? Did Andy? And how is that tied to your corpse?"

"Andy did know and it's not my corpse and I'm not sure how it might be tied or who killed him. His name was George Gentry, apparently, and he was undercover for the Mounties."

"Ah. So they were investigating me?"

"Not that I know of. Andy didn't tell me everything. They aren't even sure that the maple syrup is coming here, just that Canada has a huge maple syrup leak going on and they suspect it's coming through Bangor and then Abigale before being moved on."

"Maple syrup leak. That's a good one." He smiled and waited for Annie to match the smile.

Her half grin released his hunched shoulders.

Tom shrugged. "Look. Get ahold of Andy. I'll tell him all I know, which isn't much. I never thought about smuggling. I should have known something was up. I didn't think about something coming in from Canada. I'm sorry."

The Chilled Corpse

"So now tell me about what Marc and Annette want to store."

"Oh, that. Yes. They run an antique business, as you know. Some high end stuff, with a lot of it online. They've been renting a storage unit in Bangor, but that's expensive and inconvenient. Or so they say. It's a legitimate business, Annie."

"I'll let Andy know you would be willing to talk with him. Meanwhile, we've signed with Marc to use the barn. Just, help me keep an eye on it, to be sure it is being used for the wrong thing. Same for John and Joanne."

"Yes." He hung his head, nodded. "I'm sorry." He looked up. "All forgiven?"

"Maybe. I'm not even sure that was tied to the murder."

"Of course. Anything else?"

"No more secrets. And I do appreciate the help since I've been here. It's all a mystery."

Annie left, not convinced Tom had told her everything, but reassured that he'd talk to Andy if the opportunity arose. She returned home and sat on her rock by the lake, thinking about changes in her life, and more to come. It would be nice to have the industrious John and effervescent Joanne around. That would discourage people from taking advantage of an empty and derelict property. The property hadn't been entirely neglected, though, when she'd arrived. Could she trust Tom in the future? She thought so. What a weird world she was in. Dead people, smugglers, a huge house, and money to burn, and an attractive Mountie thrown in the mix.

The bright fall colors of the trees around the lake made her wish she could paint. She pulled her phone and took some pictures but was disappointed that they didn't seem to catch the vibrancy. Maybe there were photographic tricks to getting the colors right. She'd ask Julie.

With a huge sigh, she stood and went into the house.

The small-town closeness both warmed her heart and set off a sense of being caged. Everyone knew what everyone was doing. So how did smugglers get away with bringing in truckloads of maple syrup, store it for six months, haul it off and no one seemed to know about it?

After a few hours in the library with pen and paper, drawing up questions about the mystery, the train of thought bled into questions to ask Julie at the paper about anything untoward, like maybe rented trucks coming through town and getting in accidents.

Onto her list, she put "law enforcement" with a question mark. Perhaps somebody had taken bribes to look the other way. It could be Dave or Chet or anyone of the other half dozen officers in the county.

Someone somewhere knew something or observed occurrences out of the ordinary. Surely, in a small town, where everyone knew everything, she could ferret something out.

Throwing her pencil across the room in frustration, she went for an evening snack, watched a program on PBS about bats and snakes and went to bed.

Her night was filled with bats that drank from large barrels and cigarette boats ferrying illegal whiskey by men dressed like 1930's gangsters.

Wednesday morning, after her restless night, Annie tried to slow her roll, but still got to the newspaper office before Julie. She had her list of questions in hand.

The Chilled Corpse

"Got a major accident outside Bangor. Want to tag along and see how to get information?"

"Sure."

The two women got into Julie's car.

As soon as Julie put the car in gear, Annie pulled her list out. "I have some questions to ask."

"Shoot. I'll answer what I can."

"What do you know about Tom?"

"There's a question I didn't expect."

"And---"

"Brought up in Abigale, went off to law school, was expected to take over Peters' and Son law practice when he came home, worked with his dad for a while, but that didn't work out. He was only a mediocre lawyer because his heart wasn't in it. His friend Joe, on the other hand, was eager and well suited to it. Now, Tom writes books. Good ones, from what I've heard, and they sell well, I guess."

"Anything else? Ever been in trouble with the law?"

"No. Tom. Heck no. Well, not that I know of. Maybe during his college years when he was away. I wouldn't know about that, would I?"

"You'd say clean cut and law abiding?"

"You 'know' him."

"I just met him, actually. You know I'm new to all the secrets of this town."

"There's a book. Written during the late '80's I think. It details the history, good and bad, of this town. I think it was done by Claire's mother. For instance, this town was a byway for booze during Prohibition. Quiet, out of the way, with the lake on one side and the river on the other for quick getaways, and it seems that for that same reason, it was a way station on the underground railway during slave days."

"I guess I need to get my hands on a copy. Was the Dower House mentioned, the original builders, and the Weeks family?"

"Your relatives may not have been squeaky clean, you know. Are you sure you want to delve into that?"

"I am. I want to know. I've already learned my family history wasn't what I thought."

"Sure, sure. Tom is good folks, though." Soon they were at the accident scene. Annie watched Julie camera hanging from a strap around her neck, casually speak with responders working the accident. After watching for a bit, she went to work taking pictures of the mashed-up cars, in awe that no one was killed.

Back at the office, Julie went right to work on the computer, glancing at her handwritten notes. After five minutes, she glanced up. "Thanks for the pictures. I'll inspect them after transcribing my notes. Thanks for the company."

After being dismissed, Annie left. Where to now? Maybe she'd go talk with John. If he'd been around like Tom suggested, he may have seen something, some sort of thing that could lead to who was behind all this.

= = =

Chapter 24

The hardware store was not busy. John was nowhere to be seen, though. Joanne greeted Annie with enthusiasm, until she asked about John.

With a deep sigh, she finally answered. "He's finally gone off to the doctor. I've been after him for weeks. He has a boil on his neck."

"Oh, sorry."

"How can I help?" She waved her hand to indicate the store. "I know about as much about this as he does and can locate stuff faster."

"Not about hardware, I'm afraid. I just want to talk to him about what he may have seen around my property. I'm told he's been out there fishing often."

"He didn't think there'd be any harm in having his boat there, with no one around." Her brow wrinkled with puzzlement. "I'm sure you don't mind that he was there before you came up." She leaned further across the counter. "He did remove the boat when he heard you were arriving to take possession. Tom told him he'd found you."

"Yes. No, I didn't mind. I just want to know what he may have seen. Seems he wasn't the only one using the property."

"Well, no. I guess once in a while some locals would go out there and go swimming."

"Tell him I'd like to talk with him, would you?"

"Will do."

"I know. Why not come out to supper tomorrow night?"

"I'll tell him you've been around asking." She looked away, disengaging from the conversation. "Have a good day, then." She glanced back at Annie, then turned and walked to the back.

What now? Annie went home and didn't know if she ought to prepare for guests for supper the next day. She sat for a while by the lake before going in.

The list prepared the day before haunted her. What did not make the list that was important? What was being missed, by her, by Andy and others? What was the key?

Joanne called to say they'd gladly come out to supper. Annie popped some chicken breasts out of the freezer to thaw for a slow cooker recipe she'd seen in a magazine.

With thousands of volumes in her library, she wondered if she had that history of Abigale already. She perused the shelves. The ladies might have acquired a copy. It might be a great idea to index the books and digitize the list for easier access. Maybe Marc and Annette could look it over and see if she had any real valuable books.

The next evening, the table was set, and the meal was ready, just being kept warm. The phone rang and it was Andy, checking in.

"I've got a list of questions I'll be asking folks. Are you really a police officer, though? Were you really on duty when you came here?"

"What a question," responded Andy. "And the answers are yes and yes. And you aren't supposed to talk about that to anyone."

"Too late. And I'll talk to others, too, but only Julie and Tom know you were a policeman."

"I don't suppose you got anyone approach you about using the space?"

"The town accountant Marc and his wife run a weekend antiques and auction house and they'll be using my barn. Tom set it up. And speaking of Tom, he says he used to let this Bangor outfit, or what he thought was a Bangor group, use my barn for storage, back before I arrived. He says he'll speak with you and tell you all he knows, which isn't much. He also says he never knew what was in those small blue barrels."

"Small blue barrels? Doesn't sound like what I'm looking for."

They chatted a few more minutes. "Oops, gotta' go. Have a good evening."

"I will. I have company coming in. They'll be using the boat house for their yard sale business."

Andy didn't even ask whom and sounded distracted. "Talk to you later." He hung up before she could say goodbye.

Supper went well. Joanne had brought chocolate cupcakes for dessert. John led the conversation, telling tales of fishing on the lake from the time he was very young.

With the coffee and cupcakes, Annie pulled her list of questions. "Did you ever see trucks bringing in anything to the property? Did you ever hear rumors about anything going on here? Did you see strangers hanging around town?" Twenty questions in all, most of which sounded repetitive as she asked them.

Finally, putting down her now empty cup, Joanne spoke up. "Why the grilling? Something happen? Is this related to the dead guy at Josie's?"

"Thanks for not asking about '*my*' dead guy."

"Welcome. Now, what's this about?"

"I'm not at liberty to tell you much. It does seem this property may have been used for some illegal purposes."

"Right. Well, there've been rumors for decades, of course." Joanne toyed with her empty plate and utensils. "Some suspected that this house was part of the smuggling of Canadian whiskey during Prohibition and even later, sneaking the Canadian whiskey into the US to avoid tariffs. This has never been proven. Might just be rumors, you know." The comment was punctuated with a smile.

"Will you tell me if you hear of anything."

"Sure," responded John. He nodded at Joanne and pushed back from the table. "We'll let you know."

Almost like scared rabbits, the two were out the door, leaving Annie wondering if she had hit a nerve, if they knew something they weren't speaking about.

The next morning, Annie reviewed the list of questions as she drank her coffee. What had triggered the couple to bolt? Which questions were redundant? After an hour, frustrated with the list, she stepped outdoors. She went to the barn and poked around into the corners and under the shelves and in the loft. Piles of rope, empty wooden barrels, a pile of old horseshoes in one corner, various tools, bits and pieces of wood, boards, and more, but nothing with any clues of previous use of the building other than things showing it was once used as an animal barn.

Next, she went to the boat shed. It had been cleaned out by Joanne when she painted it and there was a small pile of odds and ends in one corner: oars, several fishing rods, a fishing

The Chilled Corpse

tackle box, which she found empty, a small coil of rope and two different metal anchors.

By this time, she was feeling chilled and went back to the house. Where might she find any history of the house? Maybe the journals. After a small lunch, she sat with a pile of the older journals. She'd found that Kellie Marie was more open in her posts, so she started there. Hours later, she knew nothing more than when she started, except that the people in this house were never concerned with money and had done elaborate parties with many overnight guests until the late 1970's. Little was mentioned about the property. Apparently, the ladies never mowed the lawn or went fishing or dug around in the garden.

Her next move might be to talk with Marc and Annette. Maybe she'd start with Annette and see if she'd be open about their plans for the use of the barn. She honed her list of questions a little more, gathered her courage and headed over e Marc's accounting office and Annette did his reception work. She found Marc alone in the office.

"How can I help you? You need help keeping track of all that money you'll inherit?"

"Geez, that's a lead. No. I know we have a signed contract for you to use my barn for storage."

"Are you rethinking loaning it to us? You think you want more?"

"No. I just was wondering what sorts of things you'll store there."

"Oh, well, we won't know until we have it."

Sensing his hostility, she decided to curtail the list of questions. "Like what, though. Will it be any sort of perishable?"

"No. Mostly furniture. We carry our own insurance plan, if that's your worry."

"No." A deep sigh escaped. "Look, I'm not trying to back out of our deal. Just, it seems the property may have been used for illegal things in the past. I'm just trying to avoid any of that."

"Yes. Well, I do know some kids have gone out there necking and drinking and smoking pot. The cops route them out from time to time. I know that John from the hardware kept a boat out there, and sometimes some towns folks 'borrowed' it." His look was challenging.

"No, not like that. Like, maybe someone was storing things there."

"Drugs?"

"No, I don't think so." To lighten the mood, she repeated what she'd heard. "Back in the day, maybe it was used to store illegal whiskey from Canada. You know, during Prohibition."

"That was an odd time in history. Drinking carried on as before, just it was a little trickier to get. Drunks will be drunks."

"Yes. Well, I guess I agree."

Marc had successfully derailed her whole line of questions. Was he hiding something?

He continued. "Look, we'll use it mostly for large furniture items. The valuables are kept in our safe, and the books we

The Chilled Corpse

might acquire are kept at our house where we can keep them free of dampness and infestation."

"Good, then.. I should have asked this before. I just didn't think." She stood to go and turned to the door.

"Just to reassure you, we won't be storing any illegal things, and thanks for letting us have the rental."

Annie nodded without turning to him, and left, feeling the trip had been wasted, but also that he knew something. She just didn't know how to pull it into the light.

= = =

Chapter 25

On Friday, Annie turned up to do her part in distribution of the bi-weekly paper. After the papers had been dealt with, they went to Josie's again, for a good dose of coffee and a light brunch. Josie wasn't busy and sat with them for a full half hour.

"How's the rental's going?" asked Josie as she set the plates and coffee carafe on the table.

"Oh, rentals? You renting out rooms?" Julie put down her cup and stared at Annie.

"Does everyone know everyone's business?" asked a frustrated Annie.

"Of course," responded Josie. "It's our hobby."

Julie chuckled. "For you. For me, at the paper, it's my job."

The dichotomy of the two women's perspective on gossip relaxed Annie as they all had a quiet laugh.

Julie folded her napkin. "Seriously, though. How's it going?"

"I've got someone who will be doing yard sales of antique tools and such. And then I have someone who will be storing the odd pieces of furniture for their business." Annie took a deep breath and explained who would be doing what.

"I know that John had a boat out there and they took it out when they heard you were arriving."

"Yes. I'd heard. He's asked permission to have a boat there again, and he'll build me a dock. They'll be closing the store come the New Year, retiring, you know, and they'll be doing a yard sale sort of thing from the boat house. Joanne has already painted the interior."

The Chilled Corpse

Julie nodded at her. "Good for you. I'll be glad to see more people around that place."

"More people?" It wasn't a question, but a possible lead, lighting up an idea for Annie. Had John seen people around the place while fishing? Did John know someone who was using the place and didn't want to tell on them? "Been nice, ladies, but gotta' go." She used a local expression she'd heard. "Gotta' see a man about a horse."

She left Josie but went to the hardware store. Joanne was out but John was there.

"John. What are you not telling me?"

He turned partially away, pretending to be rearranging a display on the counter. Then he turned back, but still didn't look up, keeping his hands busy with a display of nicknacks between them.

Annie waited for the fidgeting to stop.

Finally, John looked at her. "I'll tell you. But I don't think it's connected to that man's death."

"Go, then."

"When I'd go out there fishing, sometimes some people would come out swimming or picnicking or something. They got so used to seeing my car there that no one paid any mind. The odd person out was the guy in the Border Patrol car. I didn't pay much mind to him either. He apparently was out there to eat lunch. They sometimes come into Bangor for court cases, you know." He paused and rearranged one small item, moving it an inch. "So, sometimes he got out of his car and sat by the lake, as if watching me. I didn't mind that, either. I only pay attention to the game wardens, but I always have my license."

"Go on. Something more?"

"Yes. He started parking near the barn out there. And getting out. He went into the barn once or twice." He nodded and stopped fiddling. "So, after he was gone, I went to the barn and looked. It was locked up. I peered in the window. If it was locked and he'd gone in, he had the key. There were stacks of blue barrels. Not the large fifty-five-gallon ones, but smaller ones. I thought that odd. I'd never seen anyone in there." He waved his right hand, then his left. "I watched more closely after that. He didn't always go in. But I did see tire tracks to the barn after a rain. I could see the grass was worn from regular use." He shrugged. "It was none of my business, of course. I knew it wasn't illegal drugs, not in small barrels like that. And if Border Patrol was involved, well, it must not be anything illegal. Maybe he had some personal stuff going on in there. Potatoes are big in Maine. The barrels were always gone each year before the hard freezes of November."

"You're thinking someone was storing potatoes, from spring to fall, in my barn. How does that figure?"

"Now that you mention it, doesn't make sense, does it. It wouldn't have been potatoes, I guess." He rearranged some things he'd already moved. "Look, the man stopped and spoke to me once or twice. The first time, he was waiting for me as I came in off the lake. He'd just been sitting there waiting. His name, he said, was William, but the name didn't roll off his tongue easily." He paused, his brow furrowed.

"Go on."

"Anyways, this William, no last name, in the Border Patrol car, he asks questions like how often I'm fishing, did I ever fish in the evening or at night."

The Chilled Corpse

"Who would fish at night?"

"Well, in the summer, you might go hornpouting." At her puzzled look, he explained. "It's a bottom feeder that bites best after dark. A small catfish. But that would be like just after dark, not into the night."

Annie nodded. "You saw this guy who called himself William, who was around my barn. Funny, but Tom never mentioned it."

"Tom was not around much, just coming up to mow and stuff. He may not have noticed the barn was being used. Or he may have, I don't know." He toyed with small items on the counter some more. Then he looked up. "Honestly. You'd have to talk with him. I just know what I saw, and that wasn't much. But someone was using the barn. I spoke to this William character a few other times, but only saw him go in the barn like twice."

"And you never saw anyone else?"

"No. No one else."

"Thank you for being up front with me, then."

"I'm not in trouble with you?"

"This was all before my time, wasn't it? If you happen to see this William again, though, please let me or Sheriff Dave know? That's where I'm headed next. He may have questions for you, but you don't' seem to know much." She started to turn, stopped and turned back to him. "If that really is all you know."

"Oh, it is. I'd tell, if I knew anything. You think it might be connected to, you know, the Josie's Inn thing?"

"Well, I purely don't' know."

"Am I still going to be able to use the place for our flea market?"

"Yes. It might be a good idea to have more traffic around the place. Have a good day." Annie left the store and went to see the sheriff.

Chet greeted her like a long-lost friend. "So glad to see you, young lady." That was odd since Chet was probably her own age. "What may I do for you this fine day?"

Images of Chet trolling in a garbage dumpster chased across her mind. She smiled at him. "Sheriff in?"

"Sure."

Apparently, the sheriff had heard her as he came out into the hallway. "Right this way, young lady," echoing Chet's greeting, and then she knew where Chet had picked up the habitual greeting.

She repeated all she'd learned from John.

"We'll look into it. Leave it with us. But you think Tom didn't know the barn was being used?"

"He knew. He just didn't know for what. Or at least, that's what he claims. I purely don't know."

"We'll interview him, for sure." He stood and motioned her to the door in a dismissive gesture. "Leave it with us," he repeated. "I doubt it's connected with the dead man, though."

Annie left, feeling the sheriff knew more than he was saying.

The coming weekend seemed to stretch out before her. She felt unsettled, restless and displaced. George Gentry. Mountie. Did he leave family behind? Everyone seemed to have family but her. Josie and Tom had gotten to be dear friends, but what were they not telling her?

She felt more isolated than she had in a very long time, maybe since moving to the city. Who could she trust? Should she call Andy? Could she rely on him? Was he even who he said he was? She had no way of knowing.

That evening, she googled RCMP. She poked around on the site. She learned what they were all about and eventually came to pictures of different groups, and there, staring her in the face was Andy. Well done. He was a Mountie, then. She went to bed that night still unsettled, but a little more comfortable with some of the information she had.

In the morning, after breakfast, she dialed Andy.]

"Something wrong? Something happening?" He sounded alarmed.

"No. I just wanted to get you caught up." She then repeated what she'd learned from John, and that she'd told the sheriff about what she'd learned."

Andy huffed when she mentioned others.

"I didn't tell them about you, about who you are."

"That's good. So, Border Patrol, you say."

"That's what John said. They probably won't be around, now that I'm here."

"I'll look into it." He sounded distracted. "Talk to you later." He hung up.

"Later," Annie said to herself. "Everything is later."

She had lunch and went into the library. She skimmed more the journals left there. There were no comments that the property was used by anyone else, but then, the ladies seldom mentioned the grounds except in the context of entertainment. A picnic in the back yard, a swim party at the shore, a tea party in the garden, cocktails on the front of the house on a particularly warm August evening, and a short walk along the lane. There was not even mention of the grass being cut or the garden being tended.

Annie had a sandwich and fruit for supper and went to bed early, bored with herself but still feeling she was missing something important.

= = =

Chapter 26

John had said that the barrels that were stored in the barn were usually gone by late fall. That meant there would not have been any this year, nor would there be any coming in. With this assurance, Annie relaxed about illegal happenings around her.

The week progressed, but the more time that lapsed, the more she wondered just how much Tom had known about what was going on and why he'd never even mentioned that someone was using the barn. He'd had management of the property, mowing, and such. He had to have seen that someone was on the property, that something was being stored here. Didn't he ever wonder what?

William from Border Patrol. Not actually seen bringing anything in or out but seen going into the locked barn. That evening, she googled Border Patrol, to see what they actually did.

- Watching the border and standing guard
- Detecting, tracking, and apprehending suspected smugglers and illegal border crossers
- Gathering intelligence
- Using electronic surveillance equipment and responding to sensor alarms
- Performing traffic observations and checkpoints
- Performing city patrols and other law enforcement duties
- Writing reports

- Making arrests

So anti-smuggling was part of their duties. William of Border Patrol. Was that his real name. John had said the person stumbled on the name. Maybe he was used to being called Bill or Will?

The inconsistencies troubled her. John would have no reason to tell her a tall tale about stuff stored in her barn. Tom had no reason not to tell her about things that happened on the property before she had taken it over.

Annie returned to Josie's that evening. Josie was cleaning up after a small supper for her tourists. Fall foliage usually gave her a full house. "Mind if I work while we talk?"

"Let me help."

The two chatted about tourists, fall foliage, the lakeside, the high school football team and then Annie turned the conversation to Tom.

"Successful as an author, it seems, though most don't know that, not so great a lawyer, apparently. His heart just wasn't in it."

"I feel he isn't telling me as much as possible about the property."

"Which one? Oh, yours" Josie had been hand washing some pots while Annie put silverware into the dishwasher.

"Yes, mine. Are there others?"

"Yes. Tom owned a good deal of acreage at one point. He sold it off shortly after his father died. It netted him a goodly sum. That's where the retirement home now stands."

"Peltier Retirement? I thought he was getting his money as a successful author."

"Yes." Josie focused on scrubbing her pot extra hard. "On both counts."

Annie stopped and stared at her. "So, he wouldn't need any money for anything?"

"No."

"Was he always law abiding?"

Josie stopped scrubbing and wiped her hands on a towel. "Like what do you mean?"

"Like did he smoke pot, before it was legal, or bring in Canadian whiskey, anything like that?"

"No. Not the Tom I know, anyway. I don't know how he was when away at college, but as far as I know, he was always a straight arrow. Why the twenty questions about Tom?"

"Something just isn't right about something. John told me a story about stuff stored out in my barn every year, well, except this year, apparently. Why hasn't Tom spoken about it."

Josie took a big breath and let it out. "Look, you weren't here. The place was empty. He had charge. What if he loaned out space?"

"It's t just that he never mentioned it. I'm just trying to figure out why.

Josie bobbed her head. "Just let the past go, Annie." She turned back to the sink and took up her task with the pots. "You are from away, right? You have no idea how small towns work. But the Tom I know, and have known all of our lives, he wouldn't have anything to do with anything illegal. Just leave it alone."

With a silent sigh, Annie finished loading the dishwasher and turned to Josie. "Gotta' go. Take care. Good luck with your tourists."

Josie turned to the retreating Annie. "Don't go off all mad. I know the transition has been stressful for you. Patience with us small town folks."

Annie turned at the door. "I'm not an idiot, Josie. I'm just trying to get caught up on events. That's all." She walked out and went home.

Sunday, Annie lay abed longer than needed. She contemplated her perception of John, Josie, Tom and even Joe. Factor in the Border Patrol, and it was a mystery. She was up and fixing coffee when her security system told her someone was in the yard. She picked up her phone and looked. Four people in a car. Massachusetts plates. Probably a tourist. She watched the car as she finished coffee and breakfast. The people got out, took pictures, got back in the car and left.

Shortly thereafter, another car came in the yard. She recognized Tom's car, and shortly there was a knock on the door.

"Hey, smells like fresh coffee."

"Come in. Yes. I thought at first you were another tourist."

"Maybe put up a sign 'private drive'?"

"Maybe. Had breakfast? Frozen waffles or toaster pastry."

"Actually, I ate at Josie's, and she says you have questions."

"Yes. I guess maybe I do." Taken aback by his bluntness, she served him a cup of coffee. "Tell me about the use of the barn."

The Chilled Corpse

"Uh, it wasn't used this year."

"But it was used in past years. And you never thought to mention it."

He sipped his coffee and carefully put the cup back on the table. "All right then. Here's the scoop. We didn't know if we'd ever find an owner. Here was this building standing all empty. I was approached about it. I said I guessed it was all right. They were willing to pay rent." He held his hand up. "I never benefitted from it. All that rent money, it went directly into your accounts."

"So why would you not tell me about this?"

"I just didn't think it would concern you, is all."

He sipped on his coffee a little more, but held the cup, cradling the cup against his chest. "I don't know who stored what. It was locked. When I looked in through the windows, there were some blue barrels. That's all I know."

"No. You need to tell me who approached you."

"Annie, I don't need to tell you anything." He made as if to stand, then relaxed back into the chair. "Sorry. I'll tell you that it must have been legitimate, because the request came from Sheriff Dave. I didn't give it a thought. And it wasn't drugs or anything. He wouldn't, you know."

"So, the sheriff asked to store stuff in the barn, it got locked, and then the stuff, whatever it was, vanished in the fall?"

"Yes. That's about right."

"And you never saw anyone around?"

"No. I wasn't here a lot, you know."

"But was it the sheriff renting it?"

"No. He was asking for someone else. A friend, he said."

"Thanks." Annie smiled at him, not sure if he was telling the whole truth, but trying to let him know she appreciated the information.

"So, want to go on a small road trip tomorrow? We'll go on a sightseeing loop through this grand state you've moved to. Most of the foliage up country has moved beyond peak stage, but coastal areas will be bright and beautiful."

"I'd like that. I haven't had much chance to see the coast." She relaxed. This was the Tom she knew; congenial, easy, eager to please. The phrase 'easy to please' might explain the reason he had allowed her property to be used by someone he didn't know for something he didn't know about. Or did he. She continued smiling as he bid goodbye, forcing herself to be cordial, but a smidgeon of doubt lingered.

Monday morning, Annie climbed into Tom's car for their trek along the coast. She was excited. She'd heard of the wonders on the Maine coast and looked forward to the day. Tom had promised to bring snacks and drinks and said they'd eat lunch along the way.

As they rambled along narrow country ways, smelling salt marshes, exploring deserted beaches and lighthouse properties, Annie immersed herself in the enjoyment of the beauty and a well-informed and affable guide. They had a seafood platter at Moody's Diner, a landmark along Route 1, Maine's coastal highway.

Darkness was making itself known by the time Tom dropped her off at her house. "Thanks, Tom. I had a grand day."

"Me, too. You are easy to be with."

"I'll remember this day."

The Chilled Corpse

"Yup. Last hurrah before the nasty weather locks us inside."

"For sure. Have a good night, then."

"I will, and you too."

Back in the house, Annie allowed her doubts about Tom, and others in the community, to surface, again. Sleep came with some difficulty.

Tuesday dawned dark and rainy. Delivery of papers would be damp. She reluctantly went to work, images of her adopted state seashore dancing in her mind.

= = =

Chapter 27

After the deliveries, as the two were enjoying coffee and a pastry, Josie overheard Julie ask Annie about the dead man, as she was setting up a luncheon. "I wish everyone would just forget it and move on. When will you cover another murder in your paper, Julie?"

Julie had been sipping her coffee and spluttered. "More like when was the last time, before this one?"

"Yeah, that too. Can you dig up something exciting to take people's minds off this?" Julie rubbed at the same spot on her counter, over and over.

"I would if I could. You know, the news is fleeting. But I won't manufacture it, like the internet does." She finished her coffee. "Well, off to the world of 'real' news, then. Maybe there'll be a spectacular crash or something." She pushed back from the table but didn't stand.

"Maybe there'll be some incident of smuggling or something," added Annie out of frustration.

"Smuggling?" Josie giggled. "My grandfather used to smuggle. Good old Canadian Whiskey. He'd bribe the border guards, bring it in on the river, or even run it down the Golden Road."

"Golden Road?"

Julie wiped her lips with her paper napkin and nodded. "There's a road running deep in the woods. It's not an official Maine road. It's mostly for loggers and maintained by them but runs right up to the border and maybe over it, and no one monitors it. Well almost no one. Hunters, deep woods campers, hikers and bootleggers use it."

The Chilled Corpse

"Well, that sounds interesting." Annie swigged the last of her coffee. "I'll have to look that one up. You can Google anything these days."

Julie had no assignments, so by lunch Annie was back home. She went to her computer and googled a Maine map. First, she traced the route she and Tom had traveled the previous day. She could see where they had gone down some peninsulas and back up. Many places, though close together, didn't have roads because of inlets. Maine had a very convoluted coast, and she could see where smuggling by boat would have been simple. Then she looked up the gold road. Wikipedia gave her an answer.

The Golden Road is a 96-mile (154 km) private road built by the Great Northern Paper Company that stretches from the St. Zacharie Border Crossing to its former mill at Millinocket, Maine.

The road, which parallels the West Branch of the Penobscot River, was built between 1969 and 1972 to bring raw wood to the mill from the company's 2.1 million acres of woodland in the Maine North Woods. Before the road was built logs were floated down the river to the mill.

Great Northern had always allowed private drivers access to the road (except for the portion next to the mill) and it is a major thoroughfare into the North Woods for sportsmen and white water paddlers on the Penobscot

Her first thought was that while politicians were wrestling with the idea of building a border wall along the southern border, Maine not only had hundreds of miles of unsupervised borders and coastline, but even had a road from the Canadian border into the heart of Maine. Her second thought circled the idea that Border Patrol were in an excellent position to smuggle goods into Maine. Is that what had been going on? Had it been drugs? Property and personal goods can be confiscated if associated with drugs, she knew. Might she lose her property?

"Just have to make sure no more happens here," she told herself.

Wednesday morning, she thought she'd go 'chat' with Dave. Maybe he didn't know what was stored, maybe he did. But at best, he could tell her who had requested storage. What did he know? Would she be poking the bear by asking?

Tom was in his car coming down the drive when she stepped out of the house.

"We need to talk," he said to her, having rolled down his window. "Want to get in. It's a bit chilly to sit by the lake."

Annie slid into the passenger seat and waited.

He gave her a half grin, then looked at the lake while he spoke. "I thought the contents of the barn might be sketchy. I went in through a window, once. Whatever was in the barrels wasn't liquid. I popped one of the spouts. It looked like sugar. Brown sugar. I didn't dare taste it. I supposed it was sugar storage for some of Dave's family, who have a bakery. Maybe they got good deals for buying in bulk. Maybe lots of things. I didn't question it. Now you are. I'm afraid for you. Is that why you put up all the security? Did Andy suggest you do that? Does he know something?"

"All these questions. Why now?"

"Because I don't want you going any deeper with this. If it's tied to that dead man, this could be dangerous." He hung his head, then rubbed his eyes with his palms. "Look, I'll go see Dave. I'll find out what he knows and who put it up to him."

The Chilled Corpse

"I know who did. It was a William, or Will or Bill from Border Patrol."

He stared at her for a full minute. "How do you know that?"

"Asking questions. Which you seemed reluctant to do." She looked out at the lake, and then after a short pause, turned back to him when he was silent. "Sorry. When I asked John some questions, he told me William sometimes hung out here and was seen going in."

"So, the mystery deepens. What would they be involved in? What would be possibly smuggled from Canada? Whiskey can't be dehydrated." He took his turn staring out at the lake. "Brown sugar can be used to make rum, I think, and the British used to have the lock on the molasses trade. Oh, gosh. Maple syrup can be sugared. It's tricky. You have to be careful not to burn it. You need dehydrators, not evaporators." With big eyes, he looked at Annie. "That's why Andy was here. That's what was in those barrels. And it is probably just the tip of the iceberg, then. Not just a few barrels gone missing, but lots of it gone missing."

"That's the story he told."

"I'll be. I just didn't see any harm in using the barn for storage. Seems I should have asked more questions."

"I'm going to go quiz Dave next. I already have a good part of the puzzle solved."

"Don't." he almost screamed it. "Look," he said more softly. "Whatever was going on, a man died. We have to assume they are connected, right?"

"Yes. But it has to end. I can't live always on edge like this."

"Granted. All right. We'll go to Dave together, then. Are you supposed to be anywhere right now?" He scrubbed his chin, then stared at her. "I know he's in this morning."

Annie nodded. "Let's then." She put on her seat belt. "Let me do the talking, though. He might be less on his guard with me, just a woman, and from away."

"He always did have a soft spot for women." He grinned and then started the car.

Dave was pleased to see Annie "So, what do I owe for this pleasure." His smile had faded when he saw Tom.

"We need to talk," responded Annie.

"I have nothing to say without a lawyer present." He flashed a lopsided grin at Tom. "Oh, wait, you are a lawyer. Or you were, until you coped out and started writing that rubbish."

"Oh, smart shot, there Dave. The lady wants to ask you a few questions. That's all. Then we'll leave."

"Fine. To my office, then."

As agreed, Annie took the lead. "I'm trying to get to the bottom of a story."

Dave shook his head. "I think I know what this is about. It's about that rental of your barn, isn't it?"

"Yes. Tom tells me you were the one to approach him about it."

"Yes. I was asked by a friend."

"So, not sugar storage for your family bakery?"

"No." He looked out the window, then brought his eyes back to Annie. His eyes darted back to the window as he repeated himself. "I was asked by a friend."

The Chilled Corpse

Tom cleared his throat as if to speak, but then didn't.

"A friend. Would his name be William? And he works for the border patrol?"

"How did---?"

"I'm right?"

"Yes." Dave visibly squirmed in his chair.

Annie pressed on. "Did he tell you what was in the barrels."

"No. I didn't ask. I didn't look, I never saw any barrels, I never checked. Tom agreed to the arrangement." He nodded at Tom. "That was the end of my part." He emphasized it with a strong nod, as if distancing himself from any more questions. "So, now you know. Anything else? I have a county to run."

"One more question."

Dave gave a big sigh. "How do I know William?"

"Yes. How do you know William?"

"We met in a bar. It was while my wife and I were separated, which was caused by my drinking. Go figure. We shared the odd brew from time to time."

"I understand." Annie glanced at Tom, then back to Dave. "So you were friends. But why you?"

"He just asked if I knew anyone with a place to store goods. I didn't think, at first, about smuggled goods. I also didn't question him."

"Did he have a hold on you, some sort of blackmail? Did he give any indication that this might be, oh, I don't know." She used Tom's words. "A bit sketchy, maybe?"

He picked up a pen, moved it an inch, then moved it back. "I only provided the contact. I had no idea what was in the barrels, and I surely didn't know, at first, anyway, that the barrels were smuggled into the US." He seemed near tears.

Tom took the lead. "I am as much to blame. I gave you a place to put it. I think we have what we came for. I believe you had nothing to do with the actual transfer of the goods."

"Yes. That's right." He leapt at the downgrading of smuggling to 'transfer of good'. "I had nothing to do with it. I just provided a name for a possible storage site."

"That's all we'll need for today. But if you can put us in touch with William, we'd be glad for it."

Dave wrote a number on a sticky note. He handed it silently to Tom. "You didn't get this from me?"

"We didn't get this from you," parroted Annie.

The two visitors stood and walked out.

Back in the car, Annie confronted Tom. "We were getting answers. What was that."

"He'd reached his breaking point. We were not going to get much more from him."

"All right, then. Now we go find this William."

"No. 'We' don't. I'll have a go at him, but I suspect he was just doing what Dave did. Finding a place to put stuff that was brought in by someone else. He also was putting his career on the line with this."

"Or he's a crooked cop, trying to get money with a side hustle."

"Or he's a crooked cop" echoed Tom.

= = =

Chapter 28

As they approached Annie's place, Tom broke the silence. "It may be time for you to get ahold of your buddy Andy and have him come back."

"I could. Or we could go interview William."

"No. Too dangerous. We don't know who it is that killed this Gent guy."

"You're very likely right."

"Wow. You just said I'm right?" He was grinning as he teased her and then followed her into the house. "Call, now. Make the call. I want to make sure, because we may have shaken something lose today."

"I hear you." She led him into the library and sat behind the desk.

He paced.

"Hey, Andy."

"I'll go make coffee," said Tom, as soon as he knew she had Andy on the line.

Annie explained the situation. "

"I'll be down tomorrow. I'd suggest you keep Tom with you," he said. "Tomorrow is the soonest I can get there." She ended the conversation, disappointed that it would take a while for him to arrive.

Tom came back into the library with two cups of coffee just as the door cam came to life. He peeked over her shoulder at her phone as he handed her the cup of brew.

"Border Patrol. Here! Now!" She pushed the cup a little further onto the desk. "Andy can't get here until tomorrow."

"He set this in motion. Now you could be in danger. I guess I'm to blame, too. I just never thought."

"It's fine. It'll be fine." She adjusted her phone. "Go ask him in. I've got Dave on speed dial."

She watched on her phone as Tom went out the door to the car and saw the gestures inviting William into the house. At first, he shook his head no, then climbed out of the car and silently followed Tom.

"You know Annie? Owner of this fine piece of property."

"Ma'am. Glad to finally meet you. I've come out to settle stuff. Dave told me you'd been asking questions."

"Yes. I asked him a few and I have a few for you, too." She waved him to one of the two end chairs.

"Look. I didn't know. I just never asked what was in the barrels. I was asked if I knew of a place to store stuff. So, I knew Dave and asked him if he knew of a place, and he told me to get in touch with Tom. So when I told this guy about it, he said it was perfect."

"I want to know how you knew the guy who asked for the storage, who he is."

William was holding his hat in his shaking hands and went to put it on the desk, then pulled back.

Annie took note that the hair on top was graying, and his head was shiny through the thinning areas. He was sweating just a little. She waited.

Tom shifted in his chair and reached for his cup of coffee, took a sip and put it back on the desk.

Annie blinked first. "All right. Little steps, then. How'd you meet the fella' that asked you?"

"I met him at the border." Sweat started beading on his face. "Thirty-four years I worked that border. I was always a great judge of character. I had a reputation as a bulldog and could detect contraband even the dogs might have had trouble with. I was a straight shooter."

Annie waited.

Tom fidgeted in his chair, then settled. "He would sometimes visit with me. I worked mostly night shift, and it gets lonely."

Tom prodded him a little when the silence stretched out. "And."

Annie and Tom remained silent, waiting.

"He'd come and go regularly. Sometimes in his car, sometimes in a small pick-up truck. We got to be like friends, sort of. He'd stop and visit with me, on some trips. He'd gift me with a bottle of maple syrup, or some cheese curds."

"Go on."

"He'd bring stuff for my wife, too. She's---." He hesitated, before finishing the sentence. "She's not well. He'd ask what she liked and gift it to me." He fiddled with his hat, then looked up at Annie. "We aren't supposed to accept any gifts from anyone, but this wasn't like bribes. He didn't ask for anything in return."

Tom touched his coffee cup, then left it where it was. "We get that, but how'd that turn into smuggling?" Tom was still facing him and after some silence he prodded him. "He was a friend?"

"Well, pretended to be, I guess."

"Then he asked for storage!" Tom sounded like he was cross examining a witness in the courthouse.

The Chilled Corpse

Sweat was running off William's face. "I told him I wanted nothing to do with drugs. He just said it wasn't whiskey or drugs." He again went to put his hat on the desk and took it back into his lap.

"I hear you," said Annie. "We just want to know how that happened."

"Yes. Storage, he said. Short term, and he assured me it wasn't any illegal substances."

"So, then you asked Dave."

"Yes. Dave told me about this place."

Annie was losing her patience. "You two. Really. Did you not suspect something shady?"

"No," said Tom, reaching out to his coffee, but only pushing it further onto the desk.

"No," reiterated William. "And it wasn't like a bribe or blackmail. He didn't promise me anything. He'd give me the money to pay for the rental and I'd pass it on to Dave, who had made the arrangements and who passed it on to Tom."

"When? When did this start?"

"Five years ago, I think, though he may have been storing some product, that's what he called it, *product*, some business venture he was into, he said, and I think he may have been bringing in some before he was storing stuff here."

"Why didn't you go to the authorities?" Now Annie played with her own cup of coffee but only moved it a few inches, then a few inches back.

William moped his face with his sleeve. "I only set up the storage. I didn't even know it was something coming from Canada to the US. I didn't know what was in the barrels. I picked the lock one day, though. I went in and checked. It looked like it might be brown sugar. That's not illegal? Then Dave told me a few weeks back what was in them. I could lose my job if authorities made a connection between me and those smugglers?" He looked at Tom. "I hear you're a lawyer. Can you help me? I'll probably go to jail, now or at least lose my job."

"I know a guy," said Tom. "Maybe if you work with him, help find out who killed this man, you'll get some help. Me, I'm no lawyer, much less a criminal lawyer. I gave that up a while ago."

"Oh." Visibly shaken, William wiped his face again. "This isn't about maple sugar! The dead guy? Oh, no." He stumbled over his words. "I can't talk to you. Who is the person you know?"

Tom looked at Annie, nodded once. "Come back here tomorrow, maybe?

Annie nodded. "Yes. If you come tomorrow, you can talk to my friend Andy."

"Is it true? I may be in a lot of trouble. I didn't connect him to this other thing. Well, not right away. Dave said the murdered guy was an undercover cop?"

Annie glanced at Tom, then took the lead. "That's the rumor we keep hearing."

"Is this guy you want me to meet with a cop?"

"Not in the usual sense of the word, no." Annie waved a hand in dismissive fashion. "Look, go home, get some rest, take care of your ill wife. You were brave to come in today to talk to us. We were about to try to find you."

The Chilled Corpse Page 217

Tom stood. "Good to meet you and thanks for coming to us. Maybe we can make this all go away. Thirty-four years, hunh?"

"Thanks. I'll see you tomorrow, then."

Tom walked him to the door.

"That was interesting," stated Annie when he'd reentered the library.

"We didn't learn anything that we didn't' already know or could have guessed at, though."

"That's right. Well, maybe Andy can get more out of him, then."

"Yes, maybe. Shall we go to lunch?"

"How about I fix us some. I've got some great sandwich fixings. And by the way, Andy suggested you might want to hang around until he gets here."

"Glad to. I was thinking of doing it, anyways."

The evening was long as they, watched parts of programs, not settling to any one thing. Tom spoke compulsively until Annie told him to be quiet.

Finally, Annie decided she'd had enough. "I'm going to bed. You have the green room. Try not to snore loud enough that I wouldn't hear the yard alarm."

"I'm not a snorer, and I'm a light sleeper. Bet I'd hear it before you."

"Let's hope we don't' hear anything all night. Andy will be here tomorrow."

As they were fixing coffee and a breakfast of toaster pastry, Andy arrived.

When she heard the car on the door cam, she looked at her phone and gasped.

Tom stood and took the phone from her. "Well, well. Nothing subtle about that."

Andy was in his red coated dress RCMP uniform.

Annie gave him a cup of coffee. "Want a toaster pastry?"

"Had breakfast in Jackman on my way down."

"As I told you on the phone, we expect William will be coming in today. We told him you would be here. We didn't tell him who you were, just that you were a friend, and might be able to help him out."

"No deals. I wish you hadn't promised anything."

Tom slowly put his cup onto the table and looked at Andy. "We wanted him to return. It was a lure. We didn't promise anything, just suggested that maybe you could help him out. It did seem that he knows something about the death."

"All right, then. We wait. If and when he turns up, let me do the talking."

"Will do, roger that." Trying to cover her irritation, Annie offered a coffee refill.

"I'm good," he said, holding his hand over the cup to stop the refill. "Maybe I'll interview him alone?"

"I don't think that's a great idea," said Tom.

"He was my friend," replied Andy.

"All the more reason," said Tom. "All the more."

Andy nodded but didn't say anything.

The trio sipped and ate and sat quietly for a time.

= = =

Chapter 29

Annie was staring at her phone, willing it to show someone coming into the yard, but jumped when she saw a vehicle enter. It wasn't a Green and White border patrol car, but a small red pickup truck.

"Well," said Tom.

"It's him," said Annie."

"I'll go invite him in."

A few minutes passed before Tom reentered the library, closely followed by William.

As soon as he saw the red coated officer, he turned, without a word and bolted for the door.

Annie had stood to greet her guest and chased him and caught him before he got to the door.

"You said he wasn't cops. That's a Canadian Mountie in there."

"That's my friend Andy. He'll help you if anyone can. Please, come back in. Andy is just interested in what happened to his buddy."

"I can't." William was shaking and pale.

Annie feared he'd pass out. She took him by the elbow. "Come. Talk to him. You can just see what he already knows. Tell what you know. Let him find the trail to the killer."

"I won't do it." Despite his protest he allowed her to lead him back to the library. He sat and looked straight ahead, stunned, refusing to look at the man who was very obviously in law enforcement.

The Chilled Corpse   Page 221

Tom took the lead. "Yesterday, you were telling us how you met the man who was storing things here. You said that Dave gave you my name as manager of this place, and that some storage space might be available."

William nodded. "This isn't being recorded or anything, is it?"

"No," responded Andy. "This is all off the record, for now. I'm just looking to see if the smuggling was connected to George's death."

"Oh. Yes. Well, I didn't used to think so. George. That's the dead man?"

"Yes. George Gentry."

"And he was a friend of yours?" Still shaking, William looked away, after asking the question.

"Yes. And a co-worker. He was here trying to figure out who was smuggling maple syrup out of Canada, selling it in the US. We think you can help."

"I'm not sure. He told me his name was Bruce." Gaining confidence, William continued. "I worked the border for over thirty years. I can usually spot a fraudster. I have a reputation for it. I never ever took a bribe, or let something go. This guy, he had me completely bamboozled, though." Gaining momentum, he sped on. "He would gift me things, and things for my wife. Small stuff, you know. Then he asked about storage. I knew Dave. Dave knew Tom, and the deal was done, but I never got a single penny out of it. So, I'm not part of the smuggling, am I!"

"No, it would seem you aren't." Andy spoke softly and reassuringly. "Thirty years of diligently minding the borders. You just introduced someone to someone else. That's not against the law." Then he struck as quick as a snake. "But murder, now that's against all laws. What do you know about that."

The strike hit hard. William crumpled. He broke into sobs.

Everyone else in the room just sat quietly, letting the man have a moment.

Finally, after a few minutes, William looked up, tears streaming down his face. "I guess it was bound to come out. I'll tell you, if this is off the record." He waited.

"Please, go on," said Andy, once again speaking softly.

"I've always been law abiding. I don't' approve of violence. After serving in Kuwait, I don't keep weapons in my house. My weapon always stays at work."

Tom nodded at him to encourage more. "You are doing fine."

"My wife, she's not well. She's Kuwaiti. She was in their special forces. That's where we met." He smiled for the first time since entering the room. "We fell in love almost instantly. We weren't supposed to fraternize with the locals, but it happened." He lost his grin. "I didn't realize, until she came to the US, that she was unstable. Something happened back there. Something really awful. I sometimes get little bits and pieces of it. She's not dangerous, or anything. But certainly some sort of PTSD. I can usually bring her back around to reality. Nightmares, certainly, plague us. Both of us. I understand. I had to do things over there. Well, you know. War is war." He went quiet, ruminative.

A loud bird chirp just outside the library window was the only sound for several minutes.

The Chilled Corpse

William wiped his cheeks and nodded once. "I can't lose her. But we have to deal with this. She told me to deal with this. She's waiting back home to see what happens here." He straightened his shoulders up. "We had nothing to do with that man's death. I can see now, though, that this Bruce character was smuggling in something. I had thought he was involved in some business here in the states. He never brought anything in when I was on duty, for sure. I never checked his vehicle thoroughly, though. But truckloads? No. Not on my watch."

He looked around at Annie and Tom, then back to Andy. "I may be guilty, by association, I may be guilty of bad assessment of character, but I sure as shoot am not guilty of murder. You'll have to look elsewhere for that."

Andy made a wave with his hand for William to continue but didn't say anything.

"Can I go? My wife is waiting to hear what happened."

"Go," said Andy.

Tom stood and shook William's hand. William stood, nodded to Annie and shambled out.

"That was interesting," said Annie when Tom came back in. "But if not them, then who did kill George."

Andy stood abruptly and bolted out, without a word, like a horde was after him."

Tom gazed at the empty doorway. "Maybe he knows something about what happened that he's not sharing."

"Could it be a member of his team, one of the other three?"

"Annie, for sure, anything is possible."

"Thanks for staying last night."

"I'll continue to stay if you think it's needed?"

"No. I don't want to take any more of your time. I don't think I'm in any danger. But thanks for offering."

"My pleasure. Any time. But we should stop spending nights together. People might talk." He was grinning broadly as he said it.

"Yes, there's that. Small towns. I'm learning. See your around, then."

After Tom left, Annie, now on her own, wondered why Andy had left so quickly.

= = =

Chapter 30

A few hours after Andy left, Annie got a call. Caller ID told her it was Andy.

"Sorry I left so quickly." He took an audible deep breath. "I just don't know how to tell you that sometimes when a thought occurs to me, I have to act on it right off."

"Understood," said Annie, though she wasn't sure she did.

"I'll be back in town in a day or two, but I think I may know who did it, after you dug around and ignited something, so thanks."

They chatted a bit more. "I had been so sure we were onto something with the Border Guard. But then something occurred to me. I need to backtrack and check something, but I'll be in touch."

The conversation provided no answers.

Annie went about her week, as usual, after the dynamic weekend. She did feel someone in town knew more than they were saying. Surely, someone from town was the killer, and that was a bit unnerving. Tuesday, after she returned from her delivery duties at the Abigale Gazette and an assignment at the school taking photos of the Math Club, Andy was at her house, waiting for her in his car.

Hesitantly, she approached him. "What's up?"

"Will you help me one last time?"

"Sure. Will it be the last time?" She smiled to show she was teasing.

"I hope to solve this, finally, with your help."

"I will if I can. What do you need?"

"I want you to invite the sheriff and his assistant, Chet. Have them out to supper, maybe?"

"Not tonight, I hope. Can we plan that for tomorrow?"

"Yes. That would be perfect. I have things I want to do today. I can help you tomorrow, to prep the meal and we'll discuss what I need you to do."

"Fine. Want to come in?"

"Later. I'm headed off to talk to Tom."

"I'll see you later?"

"Yes. I imagine that the green room is still available."

"Sure. Glad to have you stay over."

The day went slowly. It was too cool and cloudy to spend outdoors. Annie made sure the green room was ready for guests, then she made a menu and headed to the city for a great shopping trip. She thought meat and potatoes with a vegetable side would appeal to the men. To finish the meal, she'd serve apple pie and ice cream, and finish off with fresh brewed coffee, what she thought of as 'good old boy' fare. She also wanted some great food for this evening for Andy, and for breakfast, and she needed some cold cuts and bread for sandwiches.

Shopping done, she got the groceries in the house. Then she turned to the library and played around on the internet, returned a few Facebook comments from former associates in the city that still kept in touch, and then she cleaned, dusting, vacuuming, and rearranging the folds on curtains in various rooms, just biding time until Andy returned.

She started supper, thinking he'd arrive by evening. She was starting to think she'd be eating alone when she heard the car in the driveway. She met him at the door.

The Chilled Corpse

"Yum. Smells good. Supper?"

"Of course. Just got ready. Come on in."

The two spent a quiet evening. When Annie tried to probe Andy for his thoughts or what he'd been up to, he diverted the conversation.

"What can I expect tomorrow?"

"I expect you'll find out as I do. I think we'll learn something very interesting about the dynamic duo of your law enforcement."

"Dynamic Duo. That's precious. If they're so dynamic, why do they need you to come down out of Canada to solve this?"

"Had an interesting conversation with Tom. I had been reading his books and didn't realize it was him."

"Steam Punk. I never even knew it was a thing."

They talked about Tom for a bit until Annie wondered if it was Tom that Andy suspected of the crime, but then realized he just didn't want to discuss anything more serious than books.

"Going to bed, now, I think. Been a long day." Andy stood and bid Annie good night.

After he'd left, Annie sat, contemplating what the next evening might be like. Would there be hostilities? Did Dave or Chet have a piece of the puzzle? Why didn't Andy just ask whatever it was that he wanted to know?

= = =

Chapter 31

Andy did help prepare the meal. Annie had learned, during the month he had lived at the Dower House, that he was handy in the kitchen. The whole house was redolent with roasted meat when they heard a vehicle in the yard.

Andy nodded at Annie, and she met Dave and Chet at the door. They were dressed casually, as befitted a meal at a friend's house.

Andy was seated at the table when they entered the kitchen and Tom was standing beside the stove.

"Heard you were back in town," said Dave, looking at Andy. "Hi Tom. A right real dinner party, this."

Tom turned and took the open bottle of wine he'd brought and poured some in each of the glasses. "Dave, Chet. Hope you came hungry, because I saw the size of the roast."

"I'm starved," answered Chet, rubbing his stomach, as he sat and then reached for the wine glass.

Annie almost missed the look Dave shot in his direction, but not the comment.

"You're on duty, later?"

"Yes. Just a glass. Ummm, smells great and this is great wine." He quaffed it like beer.

Dave took a sip. "Yes. Fine. This is great. An old bach like me does appreciate a fine meal, for sure. It's why I eat at Josie's so much. I keep offering to marry her, but she's content to stay single, for now, anyways." He looked at Tom as he said the last.

"You know I've asked, too. Love her cooking."

Annie set out the meal, with Andy's help. Tom refilled the glasses as everyone helped themselves to the pot roast, potatoes, carrots and string beans.

"Leave room for apple pie." Annie was nervous about what might come next.

The talk around the table was general, about happenings in Abigale and the neighboring city of Bangor, as well as a few comments about statewide politics. With five people around the table and convivial conversation, soon the wine bottle was empty, and Tom reached over and opened a second one that had been tucked away on the counter.

Dave was a bit flushed. Annie wasn't sure if it was the warm kitchen of the wine. She decided it was wine as he grew more gregarious.

Dave chuckled as he addressed Tom. "I almost got you that time you and what was his name? And you had toilet-papered the gazebo."

Tom ducked his head once, then denied it. "That wasn't me. I told you that." His smile seemed to belie the statement.

"Then there was the time you and your classmates put wood blocks under the wheels of the cruiser and the tow truck driver had a great laugh at my expense when he discovered why the car wouldn't move forward. I thought it was the transmission."

"I never," protested Tom.

"No one would ever dare pull that stuff on me," bragged Chet.

Andy had been quiet for a while. His wine glass stayed untouched throughout the meal.

The pie was gone. All that remained on the table was empty dessert plates and empty coffee cups.

"Coffee, anyone. Fresh made pot."

"Oh, I will," said Dave.

"Me too," said Chet.

"I have a date with a computer. Final chapters, so count me in," said Tom.

Andy nodded yes.

After the coffee was poured, Andy spoke up. "So Chet. It's my understanding that you are the one who found the bag of bloody paper towels?"

"Yes. We sent them off to the state. They do murders in Maine. And we don't have the facilities, you know. They tested positive for that man's blood."

"So, you think he was in the room with those people he came in with?"

"Oh, sure. It looks like one of them did for him. But they scampered back to Canada, from what I can tell."

Dave shot him a look but remained silent.

"You think he came down from Canada, his companions killed him, and then they left, tucking him into the cooler before going?"

"Well, they couldn't bring him back across the border, could they? I mean, a dead man?" He took a swig of coffee and quickly put it down, clattering the cup on the saucer.

"That's only one theory," said Dave. "One of many."

Annie's eyes widened as she caught the drift of discovery.

The Chilled Corpse

Tom seemed to know what was planned. "You were on duty, that evening, weren't you?"

"Yes. I was. It's a big territory to patrol, but I do my best."

Tom pushed harder. "Does your best include a trip to Rosie's?"

"Rosie's. Yes. I went to Rosie's. She was having another of her parties. The neighbors complained about the noise, so I went to tell her to keep it down."

Dave now picked up the narrative. "Rosie's." He shook his head. "Rosie's. You didn't tell me about that. We're supposed to log all the complaints."

"This didn't come in through dispatch. Someone called me, *personally*." He patted his hip, where the cell phone was hung.

"You are now doing private law enforcement.?"

"I guess they didn't want to get her in trouble, again."

Tom nodded at him. "Understandable, since there's been some 'cease and desist' against her. So, who called you?"

"A neighbor. What's it matter to you, college boy."

"Just trying to get a feel for your whereabouts that evening."

"Well, I guess I don't have to account to you for anything."

"And did Rosie offer you some of her white lightning?" Tom was pushing on, despite the hostility.

"White---. No I don't drink that rotgut. Who knows what's in it! I only had a beer."

Dave now focused on Chet. "A beer. That's all. Just one? I'll check with her."

"Well, it may have been more than one. But I swear, I wasn't there long."

"I've warned you about drinking while on duty, Chet. Did I not tell you what would happen?"

"You can't prove I did that. I wasn't drunk. I only had a couple of beers. It was the social thing to do. I had to hang out for a few minutes to be sure the party quieted down, didn't I."

Tom chimed in. "A couple of beers. I've never known you to have a couple of beers, Chet."

"Hey, Fancy Pants, living on daddy's money, what would you know about being in law enforcement, having to earn a living? You couldn't even hack it as a lawyer. I don't even know why you bothered to come back to town." He took a healthy swig of his coffee, but his eyes never left Tom's.

Annie hated the raw venom in Chet's voice. "So, I take it you didn't go to college Chet. You've done well here in Abigale, though. People look up to you."

The attempt to placate only puffed him up more. "Darn right. Someday, I'll have Dave's job. It's written in the stars."

Andy chimed in. "You saw nothing that night. You were drinking with this Rosie. You never noticed someone watching you?"

"Why would someone be watching me? I have nothing to hide."

Andy pushed on. "George was found in the park, by his friends."

"I didn't see any friends around when I saw him skulking around my town."

The Chilled Corpse

Annie now pressed, seeing the end results of her dinner, feeling sick to her stomach at the part she was playing. "Skulking. That's an interesting word. And what did you do when you saw him skulking?"

Caught off guard, he responded immediately. "What I did? I didn't put him in the cooler. I don't know how he got there."

"But you saw him, somewhere."

"He was in the park. Like I say, he was hanging around, like some homeless person. We don't allow that here in Abigale, right sheriff?"

Dave mindlessly nodded.

Annie caught a look pass between Andy and Tom.

Annie prompted Chet. "He was in the park, you say?"

"Yes. Said some nonsense about counting stars. He was just lying on the bench, then he stood. He was tall. I was, well, of course I don't get scared."

Dave spoke. "Did you tell him you were a police officer."

Chet looked at Dave, his eyes wide and took a heartbeat to answer. "Well, of course I would have, right?"

Annie tried to calm the developing situation. "Of course you would have."

Andy wanted to ramp it up. "You actually said the words. 'I'm a police officer'?"

Chet got defensive. "Of course I did. Remind me who you are again?"

"Friend of Annie, here."

"From Canada. You wouldn't even know how the law works here, would you?"

"Maybe not, maybe so. What's it to you."

Corpse Chapter 32

Now Chet was looking flushed. He became defensive as he realized he was being cornered. "Look, the guy was lurking in the shadows. I did what was needed to protect my community. I reached for my gun, but it wasn't there. I must have left it at Rosie's, when I showed it to someone." Now he started sweating and kept his gaze away from his police chief. He looked down at his hands, toyed with his coffee cup.

Andy became the 'good cop and repeated Chet's claim. "He was loitering. He was a stranger in town. You didn't know what he was doing. You felt threatened."

"He had this big, huge knife. He'd been peeling an apple with it. Who peels an apple with a bowie knife? I asked him for it. He didn't want to give it up."

Now Dave took up the narrative, realizing the end game. "How'd the knife end up in the victim's chest, Chet?"

"I didn't stab him. It was his own knife." Chet was sweating freely. His hands were trembling as he grabbed his coffee cup and stared down into it and was silent."

Dave was half turned in his seat and staring daggers at his deputy. "How, and don't you dare try to weasel your way out of this. It was you and him. What happened?"

Chet hung his head.

Tom spoke softly into the silence. "What happened, Chet. Surely it was self-defense or something."

Chet was quiet for a moment more. His voice was soft and uncertain when he spoke to the assembled group while staring down into his coffee cup. "We tussled. I got the drop on him, gave him a big wallop on the head and he fell. He fell on the knife. I didn't kill him. He killed himself."

"That's your story?" Andy started to stand, but Annie put a hand on his wrist.

"He was just a vagrant. A nothing. Another homeless tramp. I left him where he fell." He stopped and looked up at his boss. "I'm in trouble, aren't I!"

Dave just nodded.

Andy went to stand again.

Annie clenched his wrist harder.

Andy's grief was apparent as he uttered the final words to Chet. "George was my friend. He was a good friend. He was here on assignment. You, you piece of garbage, are responsible for his death. And you just left him there." He ran out of words as tears dripped down his face.

Dave stood and turned fully to Chet. "Chet Atwater, I am arresting you in the wrongful death of Geroge Gentry." He turned to the others at the table. "Sorry. Sorry for---." He waved his hand in a circle. "Sorry for everything." He put a hand on Chet's shoulder.

Chet was now the one with tears running down his face, his head hung low.

"We'll see ourselves out. Thanks for the great meal, and sorry, again. For everything."

The three people remaining at the table were silent for a long time, looking at anything but each other.

Finally, Tom broke the silence. "Well, that's done. Well done, you two. But now I have to go to work. I have a deadline." He looked over at Andy. "Nice working with you. I may grab some of this drama for my next book. Canadian Royal Mounted Police at their finest." He stood and turned. "I'll be in touch, And Annie, thanks for a great meal, and the side show wasn't bad." He walked out of the kitchen, and they heard the front door a moment later.

"I'll be headed back tonight. Thanks for the hospitality, and the help. Now I finally know what happened. Oh, and we got the person who was bringing the maple sugar into Abigale. The lead William gave us led us to the culprits." He gazed quietly at Annie for a moment.

"My sympathy at the loss of your friend, Andy. Keep in touch."

"Thank you." Andy stood and walked out

"Well, that was different," she said to herself, as she started cleaning the kitchen. "Never expected that ending."

= = =

=== ·········=========== ========

Scan QR code to go to author page on Amazon,

The Chilled Corpse

Or go to

Amazon.com: Louy Castonguay: books, biography

Louy Castonguay

Books under Louy Castonguay

Keeper Series
My Neighbor's Keeper B07K6WQTX6
Child's Keeper B07RTPLSHR
Twins' Keeper B086KY2PCG
Teen Keeper B08FMX466K
Volunteering Keeper B091BDZLMK
Wildlife Keeper B095XQGT2N

The Lakeside Dower House Series
The Topped Toff
The Chilled Corpse
The Drowned Damsel

Aunties B&B Series
The Empty House B09B6F8VRC
The Hαllow Wall B09TV2FGYP
Weddings B0BKYPD7RC
Kinfolk B0BRQSH6LG

Books of Short Stories
Let Me Count the Ways B08T6PQVC1
Life Choices B09T8RYXYV

Books under the author name Lou Cast
Horse Rancher's Quest, B0BX72ZP6X
Erru, the Levite, BOC5S3QLYR
Maria's Choices BOCLJ3XXML

These are all available in Paperback and eBook.

For digital readers, click here **for author page for any of the books and click on follow.**

Please leave a review here, to help others find this book, if you liked it or go to author page.

Louy is a double graduate from University of Maine Farmington, a BS in Community Nutrition and a BFA in Creative Writing. She has done many types of work and now is a full-time writer.

She enjoys quilting, writing, and cooking for others, not always in that order. You can reach out to her at louycwriter123@gmail.com Enjoy this book, and the other books listed.

Made in the USA
Middletown, DE
21 December 2024